W9-ABX-515

SPECIAL MESSAGE TO READERS

This book is published by

THE ULVERSCROFT FOUNDATION,

a registered charity in the U.K., No. 264873

The Foundation was established in 1974 to provide funds to help towards research, diagnosis and treatment of eye diseases. Below are a few examples of contributions made by THE ULVERSCROFT FOUNDATION:

★ A new Children's Assessment Unit at Moorfield's Hospital, London.

★ Twin operating theatres at the Western Ophthalmic Hospital, London.

★ The Frederick Thorpe Ulverscroft Chair of Ophthalmology at the University of Leicester.

★ Eye Laser equipment to various eye hospitals.

If you would like to help further the work of the Foundation by making a donation or leaving a legacy, every contribution, no matter how small, is received with gratitude. Please write for details to:

THE ULVERSCROFT FOUNDATION,
The Green, Bradgate Road, Anstey,
Leicestershire, LE7 7FU. England.

Telephone: (0533) 364325

FOUR TEXANS NORTH

Answering a call for help from his uncle Len, Jim Rathburn drove a herd of Texas Longhorns north, into the heart of Montana Territory. It was Jim's first trip into the north country, and apart from his uncle, he knew no one there. But somebody knew him, and was waiting for him; his first night in town, two masked hombres broke into his hotel room at three in the morning, and proceeded to welcome him Montana style! When he finally came to, he found that the Rathburn name was already famous . . . and disliked.

Books by Lee Floren
in the Linford Western Library:

BLACK GUNSMOKE
LOBO VALLEY
DEADLY DRAW
THE SADDLE WOLVES
SHOOT-OUT AT MILK RIVER
RIMROCK RENEGADE
THE HARD RIDERS
RUSTLER'S TRAIL
WOLF DOG RANGE
RIFLES ON THE RANGE
GUN WOLVES OF LOBO BASIN
HIGH BORDER RIDERS
ROPE THE WILD WIND
BROOMTAIL BASIN
PUMA PISTOLEERS
THE GUN LORDS OF STIRRUP BASIN
DOUBLE CROSS RANCH
FOUR TEXANS NORTH

LEE FLOREN

FOUR TEXANS NORTH

Complete and Unabridged

LINFORD
Leicester

First Linford Edition
published November 1989

British Library CIP Data

Floren, Lee, *1910–*
Four Texans north.—Large print ed.—
Linford western library
I. Title
813′.52[F]

ISBN 0-7089-6767-1

Published by
F. A. Thorpe (Publishing) Ltd.
Anstey, Leicestershire

Set by Rowland Phototypesetting Ltd.
Bury St. Edmunds, Suffolk
Printed and bound in Great Britain by
T. J. Press (Padstow) Ltd., Padstow, Cornwall

1

Gunman's Range

THE harsh sound of knuckles hammering on the door finally dragged Jim Rathburn out of a deep sleep. The red-headed cowpuncher sat up in bed and sleepily asked, "Who's there? An' what do you want?"

"Jim Rathburn?"

Jim Rathburn's sleepiness suddenly departed. Now who on this Branding Iron range knew his name, outside of his uncle, Len? And who, beside Len, would know he was coming to Branding Iron? He had not signed the hotel register.

"That you, Uncle Len?"

The voice was deep and harsh. "Sure is, Jim. Open up, fella, an' let your ol' uncle in to see you!"

"In a minute, Len."

Still half-asleep, Jim slipped out of bed.

Moonlight came through the dirty window of the hotel room and illuminated the interior. Jim hobbled toward the door, careful not to get any slivers in his bare feet. He figured it was about three or four in the morning.

The knuckles hammered again.

"Hol' your hosses, Len."

Jim Rathburn slid the bolt and the door swung inward. The smile of welcome on his boyish face changed to a bloody smear as the fist crashed in and hit him. The blow, coming so unexpectedly, almost knocked Jim down, and it dazed him badly.

Two men, each wearing a mask, barged into the room. They were both about the same build and height, but this fact was hard to determine exactly—for each wore a long black oilskin slicker, the sleeves of each cut off to allow greater freedom of the arms.

"Work the son over, Casey!"

Jim, going backwards, smashed into the dresser. He felt the edge of the top across his back but it held him. His first thought was of his six-shooter, hanging from the post of the old iron bedstead. He made a move toward the gun—a fast and wicked lunge.

"Get him again, Casey!"

The blow came, catching Jim behind the right ear, making the world spin. He realised he was down. One man came in, boots working. The other, Jim noticed, had snagged the six-shooter. He stood there, legs astride, holding Jim's weapon. But Jim had no eyes for this man, his gaze turned to the boots that swung into his ribs with devastating effect.

He rolled over, moving away from the kicks, hit something, and realised that he had rolled against a chair, upsetting it. He came up with the chair raised, a slender man of twenty-two, dressed now only in long-handled red underwear.

The chair crashed down.

The man took it across the shoulders, and Jim heard the oilskin slicker tear. Elation flooded the cowpuncher as he realised he had hurt this man, this unknown assailant. The man grunted, went backwards, and Jim rushed him, the chair raised. Just then, something hit Jim on the side of the head. And hit him with savage precision.

He went down again, aware that the second man had slugged him with the .45. The thought came, with ironic certainty, that he had been slugged by his own gun—for some reason, the fact that he owned the .45 that had buffaloed him made him madder than ever.

"Give him the boots, Casey!"

"We'll show these Texas scissorbills they ain't got no call to come into Montana territory—"

A boot smashed in, crashing against Jim's belly. Its harsh impact knocked the wind from him. He remembered throwing another chair, but then the .45 came down again. And the next thing he knew, he was looking into a woman's face.

And a pretty face it was, too. At first because of his dazed and bloody condition, young Jim Rathburn could only remember that the face had a wide mouth, a stubby nose with a row of freckles, and that her eyes were blue—Irish blue, he thought. And her hair, was red.

"What happened, stranger?" she asked.

Jim shook his head gingerly. "They's a herd of Red River longhorns in my head," he drawled. "They're millin' around, hell for leather—Pardon me, Madam." Jim took his head out of his hands and looked around.

The room was a shambles. The dresser lay on one side, the mirror shattered, and the wry thought came to Jim Rathburn that somebody would have seven years bad luck and that that somebody might be Jim Rathburn. The thought faded almost at once, for, of all things, he was certainly not superstitious. His glance took in a chair that was now matchwood and he noticed that the carpet, which had long seen better days, was ripped in several places as the result of the melee that had occurred.

The girl was not the only one in the room. Two other persons were there—one, a heavy-set beefy woman of about forty, who held a dressing robe against her thick body; the other was an older man, who had hurriedly pulled on his pants, and was bare to the waist.

Jim said, "We woke up the whole hotel, eh?"

"*We?*" the girl asked. "Who is *we?*"

Jim grinned. He felt a little better now. "I know who *I* am," he said, "but I don't know who *we* were. If that makes sense, which I doubt."

The girl showed a frown. Despite his headache, Jim Rathburn thought the frown looked taking, for it gave her pretty face greater character. The man looked at the older woman, puzzlement on his thin features, but he said nothing.

The girl asked, "Who is *I*, then?"

"I'm Jim Rathburn, lately from Texas. I got an uncle out of this town of Brandin' Iron, name of Len Rathburn. Runs an outfit called the Buckin' Horse, I understand."

The girl's face stiffened. Jim looked at her with surprise.

"Oh," she said. "Oh."

The thick woman said, suddenly, "I'm going back to my room. This has only been a fight between those two damned cow outfits."

She waddled out, her back broad and straight.

The man said, "Me to bed. Got to get the morning stage out." He turned at the door. "The hotel clerk went after the doc, cowboy."

Then he went down the hall, leaving Jim and the redhead alone. Jim gingerly felt of his injuries. His ribs ached like there was a fire inside them. He felt a pain that made breathing difficult. His right eye was almost shut and would soon be black. His bottom lip was split but had stopped bleeding.

The girl watched him. Then she said, ironically, "Nothin' can kill a gunfighter . . . nothin' but a bullet . . ."

Jim studied her with new interest. "Why do you say that, miss. I'm no gunslinger."

"You're Jim Rathburn, you admitted."

"Yes, but does that make me a gunslinger—a killer—?"

"From what I've heard, it does." She turned to go. She had a nice back, firmly held in by her dressing robe. Jim's words stopped her in the doorway.

"Where you going, miss?"

"To my room, of course."

"Stay with me until the doctor comes. I feel kinda faint—Like I might go out of the picture—"

Her look, he thought, held scorn. "Nobody as ornery as a Rathburn can feel faint, even if slugged with a big .45. I happen to know your uncle, mister."

Jim studied her, trying to piece events together. Two masked men had entered his hotel room and knocked him cold. They had known his name and nobody but his uncle, Len, should have known he was coming to Branding Iron.

Now this woman—this pretty girl—

"What's your name?" Jim asked.

"Mary Jones, if it makes any difference, gunfighter!"

Jim didn't like the word *gunfighter*.

But he did like the name *Mary Jones*. And, despite his aching head, he managed a wide boyish smile.

"Mary Jones . . . Sure is a purty name. Mary, who was them two gents that slugged me and why?"

"You don't know who beat you up?"

"They wore masks and oilskin slickers with the sleeves cut in strips so they could hit hard. Both called the other Casey, and they knew my name."

Her blue eyes, there in the lamplight, were steady. Seriousness was on her, showing in her mouth, in her eyes.

"You're facing trouble, gunman!"

Again, that word: *gunman!* Jim shrugged it off, although it irritated him. He was no professional gunslinger. Of course, he knew how to handle a gun—either a six-shooter or a rifle, but he had been reared with guns down on the Red River. There was something here he did not understand.

"What kind of trouble, Mary?"

"Miss Jones to you, Mr. Rathburn." Her voice held icicles. "You had best talk this over with your uncle, not with me. You see, I'm only a farmer's daughter—a stupid nester's girl—One who just happened to be spending the night in the hotel, because she didn't want to drive home in the dark last evening—"

She was gone.

Jim sat there, wondering what this was all about, listening to her house slippers cross the hall. From down the hall came the sound of men's voices and the rattle of boots.

"Here comes the doc and the clerk," she called.

Jim said, bitterly, "Gee, sure nice of you to speak to me again," and then his smile widened, as he heard her door slam so hard the hinges must have jumped. To the wall he said, "A door slammer, eh? Dad used to say a door slammer was a good one to tie onto—Slam the door once hard, and she's forgot all her mad. . . ."

Three men entered.

One, short and potbellied, carried a worn bag that proclaimed him as the doctor. The hotel-clerk's eyeshade showed who he was, but it was the third man who held the attention of Jim Rathburn.

Plainly, he was an Indian. Short and heavy, with a barrel-like chest, he stood almost naked, with only a tattered pair of pants, the legs almost all gone, covering his iron-coloured body. On his feet were worn moccasins.

"I'm Doc Stone," the medico said.

Jim nodded, eyes on the redskin. He saw a wide—a very wide face—with a nose almost flat, with a scar across it. Plainly he had once received a terrible blow that had broken it. Jim saw the man's eyes were dark and big in an olive-coloured face.

He asked, "And who is he?"

The redskin said slowly, "I be Broken Nose. I be your uncle's friend, and I hear about your trouble."

"Friend of my uncle Len?" Jim Rathburn asked.

"We be friends for years. I come to

town to look for you, for Len said you come soon."

Jim liked the man. Not because he was a friend of his uncle's, but because he radiated confidence—a quiet and steady confidence. He told about the two masked men jumping him.

The doc said, "Sit still, cowboy."

Broken Nose nodded, eyes heavy. "Len an' me an' the Buckin' Horse iron—we have trouble. Texans, they move in, take our range—farmers, they come, too. Len an' me, we wait for you—"

"Where is Len now? Out at the ranch?"

The redskin nodded. "Yes, out to Buckin' Horse. Len, he sick."

Jim Rathburn studied the calm and dark face. Again, he got the feeling of bafflement, the notion that something was being withheld from him—something that was important. He sensed, somehow, that there was range war on this Montana grass. That meant plenty of trouble.

In short, things had piled up terribly quickly.

He remembered Len, his uncle. A bachelor, Len, had left Texas six years back, when he, Jim, had been just sixteen. Len had trailed north into Montana, looking for range for his Bucking Horse cattle.

Len, Jim reflected, had been built along the lines of his brother, Jim's father. Solid and tough—all man. Never a sick day in his life. Len would be about fifty-five—still tough, probably, but this Indian—this Buck known as Broken Nose—had just said that Len Rathburn was ailing.

"What kinda sickness has Len got?" Jim wanted to know.

The doctor, gingerly pressing Jim's ribs, answered that with, "The same kind of sickness you would have had, had not the racket you caused in that fight brought the clerk and other people around you so your assailants had to beat it."

Jim winced, for the man had pushed

hard on a broken rib. "And what kind of sickness would that be?"

Broken Nose answered with, "Bullet sickness. You see, Jim, your uncle Len—he get shot. . . "

2

Wild Gun Range

DAWN coloured the rangelands, lighting the cottonwood trees along the dried creek, pushing fingers of light into the big living room. It showed the man sitting there in the wheelchair, and it showed him with harsh clarity.

Jim Rathburn looked at his uncle.

Len Rathburn reminded him so much of his dead father—Len's brother—that Jim almost got the impression he was talking to his dad. The face was the same—wide and seamed, showing sun and rain, and the eyes were the same—blue Texan eyes, faded from squinting at far horizons, faded from searching for distant cattle. Eyes that could show laughter one moment, then turn to steely hardness, to death itself in the next.

"So they winged you, eh, Uncle Len?"

The man's thick lips moved. "Let me feast my eyes on you, Jim Rathburn, my only living relative—Tell me about it, son."

Jim spoke in clipped words. "The farmers moved into the Red River. We cowmen fought them—the Wire Cutters War. They hired gunmen and we matched them gun for gun. A hired killer—a professional gunman—killed my father and my only brother went after him—"

Broken Nose watched, breath making sounds in his wide nostrils. Len Rathburn's big knuckles gripped the arms of his wheelchair until the skin was clear and white.

"Go on, Jim," the cowman said.

"Ed died on the mainstreet of Latigo. I shot it out with his killer." Jim paused as memory flooded him. Two men standing there in the dust of Texas—the red Texas dust—with lifting guns. He remembered how he had gone down as a bullet seared his ribs. "He got me first, but I killed him, layin' on my belly . . . in the dust. I was in the hospital six months—infection set in."

Broken Nose's breath whistled now.

Len Rathburn said, "That left only you of the Texas Rathburns, Jim. We never knew about this until now. When did you get my letter?"

"The day I left the hospital."

"A long, long ride to Texas," Len said quietly. "I remember when I brought up my herd—across Colorady an' Cheyenne country, across the Yellowstone and the Missouri, and into Milk River. I like it here, Jim. The last of the frontier, the last open range in the West."

Broken Nose said, "A slower ride, when you come with cattle."

Jim said, "Cattle follow me, too."

They looked at him then, and their eyes held sharp questions. Broken Nose watched him, eyes dark, eyes probing. And the fingers of Len Rathburn gripped the handles of the wheelchair even harder.

"You bring up—cattle, Jim?" his uncle asked, voice hoarse.

"Buckin' Horse cattle," Jim said.

Len said, "Then you didn't sell out—sell out Buckin' Horse herds, in Texas?"

"I trailed them north. They're thirty or so miles behind us. My crew—what is left of it—is with them longhorns. No room for us in Texas. Cattle prices were low—a cent a pound on the hoof if I was lucky—so I pointed them north."

Old Len looked at Broken Nose. His eyes went back to his nephew. "We're short of range as it is, Jim. How many head you hazin' in?"

"Aroun' five thousand."

The rancher beat his fists against the arms of his wheelchair. "Tied to this damn thing for another three months, the doc says. They ambushed me, Jim, over in Chokecherry Canyon. Them damned Texans—renegados—They moved in with around eight thousand head, this last spring. Been no peace since . . ."

"Broken Nose told me, on the way out." Jim slowly expelled his breath, his broken ribs hurting him. "But he talks about like I write a letter—nobody can read it, an' he's hard to understand."

Jim showed a tight little smile. Broken Nose grinned. Len Rathburn hollered, "Squaw, bring the bottle, an' make it pronto!"

Jim heard the shuffle of moccasins from the kitchen.

"Two of them jumped me," he said. "Knew my name. Would have mebbe killed me had not a girl hollered an' they ran off."

"Who were they?" Len's voice was hoarse and anxious.

"I don't know. They were masked and called each other Casey. They wrecked the room and almost wrecked me. What puzzles me, though, how anybody knew, except yourself and Broken Nose, that I was trailin' into this Milk River country?"

Broken Nose's expression passed for the first smile Jim had yet seen on the wide face of the Sioux, but when he caught Jim's glance his face went blank. He was giving nothing away if he could help it.

Len almost groaned as he said, "Blame that on me, nephew, an' my loud mouth! Broken Nose leads me an' this rubber-wheeled hoss into a buggy, an' we goes to town—" He paused for a moment, face showing glumness. "Only man in Brandin' Iron town whatever got drunk in a wheelchair!"

Jim knew now why Broken Nose had come so close to smiling. He got a vision of his uncle, dressed in a wheelchair. Pounding the arm-rests, whisky bottle in hand. Whisky always loosened his tongue, too. And it had made even his father, who, at his best, was never talkative, a loud-mouthed boaster. Therefore Jim seldom, if ever, tasted whisky.

Jim said, "So you told about me, eh?"

"I did." Len Rathburn looked almost sheepish. "Reckon I added some choice adjectives, too, kid. Sorry I got you in a mess."

"Maybe it had to come, sooner or later." Jim was philosophical. "Anyway, I met a purty girl—a redhead—said she was a nester's daughter."

"Lester Jones' daughter, eh? Over on Willer Crick. Fine filly, that gal. But you're like all the Rathburns—women chasers."

"But I never catch them," Jim said, and grinned.

The squaw came with drinks. She was heavy and she wore an old dress, a rope around her middle as a belt. But she had a twinkle in her seamed eyes and a smile on her big mouth.

"I take care of you, my boy Jim."

Jim felt a lump in his throat. "Thanks. Your name, madam?"

"Just—Squaw. No more."

Jim replied, "Thanks, Squaw."

She looked at Len Rathburn. Her eyes danced. "He my man," she said, winking at Jim. "Me, I love him."

"Secretly," said Len, smiling, "she hates me, Jim."

The squaw's lips curled. "He no good," she said, speaking of Len. "He dumb. They shoot him—*bang*, *bang*—from saddle."

She returned to her domain, her back

broad and stout, her hips moving. Len poured three jiggers full of whisky and handed one to Jim.

Jim said, "No, thanks, uncle."

"Why not?"

"I'm a Rathburn. I can't stand whisky. It loosens my tongue."

Len studied him, said, "Quit rawhidin' me. Just one drink. To Texas, eh?"

Jim shook his head.

"Why not?" his uncle protested.

"Texas, as far as I'm concerned, is dead—a thing to be forgotten, not to be remembered."

He remembered the graves . . . the Texas graves.

His uncle's eyes were sharp bowie knives touching him. "Right you are, Jim. We drink to Montana, then?"

Jim shook his head. "No range in Montana, you tell me."

"Texas cattle have moved in, like I said. Heart Nine outfit—the figure 9, in a heart. What do we drink to, then, nephew?"

"To the North."

"Canada, eh?"

"Yes. Alberta or Saskatchewan. Open grass there, they tell me. And the Canuck gover'ment wants cattle and cattlemen."

"Hard range. Winter's tough. Cattle have to be tough."

"Texas cattle, uncle, are like Texas men. They're tough."

"You winter here on Milk River then, Jim?"

Broken Nose wheezed and it sounded shrill. From the doorway the squaw watched, attentive and alert.

"We winter here, then drive north come spring. We can't make it this fall. We have to hit in the spring so when blizzards come we have an outfit built—house, corrals, hay cut and in stacks."

"I stay here." Old Len was stubborn. "I came here first, started this outfit—those damned *renegado* Texans came later. I'll run them and the farmers out, or kill them all!"

Jim paused, holding the whisky glass. He turned it between thumb and forefinger. He had his doubts about his uncle running out the farmers. They had tried that down on the Red River. The farmers were still there, fields intact under barbwire, ploughshares shiny from turning Texas soil. But the Texas cattle had gone north. . . .

"Those renegade Texans—the Heart Nine outfit—it was they who slugged me down at the hotel, eh?" Jim asked.

"My talk must have got to them I suppose," Len replied.

"Who are they?"

"Brothers. Each about the same build and weight. But one is tougher than the other, more ornery by a long chalk."

Jim's brows rose. "Brothers?"

"One is Bowie Talbot. Other is Knife Talbot."

"Bowie and Knife? Nicknames?"

"Real names, I understand. Tough as steel, too. Why they disguised themselves—well that's plain. Sheriff down in town has been waitin' to pick them up on some charge. If he can handle them. Sheriff Harden is my man. My votes elected him."

Jim said, "I'd like to meet them again, sore ribs an' all." His grin, because of his split bottom lip, was crooked.

Somewhere, hoofs sounded. A dim tattoo against the Montana day. Len Rathburn wheeled his rubber-tired horse out on the porch, moving with great agility. Broken Nose and Jim followed. The hoofs came closer, the hill still hiding the riders. The old Texan cocked his head, listened, said, "Two riders. Maybe a couple of my men—out on bog hole riding—" He lifted his head, said, "There they come."

They loped over the hill about a quarter mile away, riding tough Montana horses. Sunlight glistened on riding gear—the silver of a mounted bit, the splash of reflection from polished spurs, the shimmer of silver-hat-band buckles.

Broken Nose said, "Them no our riders, boss."

Len Rathburn squinted, eyes hard and narrowed. "The Talbots, as sure as I'm alive. Knife and Bowie."

The riders drew closer, dust lifting. Jim

still held his drink. So did Broken Nose and Len Rathburn.

Jim lifted his glass. "To trouble," he said tonelessly.

"To trouble, Jim."

They tossed off their drinks without another word.

3

The Gun-Riders

JIM RATHBURN stood there, legs wide apart, and studied the two Talbots as they pulled in their broncs.

The steel shod hooves scattered the dust into a slow wind and then gently settled.

The brothers looked out of the same mould, even in the saddle, and it didn't need a second glance to realise they were a masterful couple who would be difficult to handle. They were dressed in rough flannel shirts and Californian pants. Each toted a couple of guns and a belt of ammunition.

Jim saw that one of them had a scar along his right jowl, a sinister disfigurement, as if a hunting knife had once caught him and cut in deeply. The rest of the face, darkly tanned, seemed to emphasise the nature of the ugly mark. The scar was something to remember, calculated Jim, as he let his hands fall to his holstered guns.

"Howdy, Len, Howdy, Broken Nose," greeted the visitors briefly and without ceremony. "Just come over to tell you we've run out a crew to build a drift fence."

They were content to ignore Jim, as though he were just a hired hand. He got the idea that this was the impression they wanted to create and not that they were aware he was Len's nephew or that they had ever set eyes on him before.

The act was good enough to puzzle even Jim, and for a moment he began to doubt whether these could have been the men who had beaten him up at the hotel. But looking them over again he realised that nowhere on the range could be found such an identical pair—in height and weight they were exactly similar.

Jim moved to one side, looking up at the man with the scar. The man's eyes, big and unfriendly, followed him, trying to show surprise. The other Talbot, apparently loafing in saddle, was looking at Len.

"Drift fence?" Len asked.

Talbot nodded. "Yes, a drift fence, Ol' Man!"

Jim noticed that Talbot's insolent manner made his uncle fairly bristle with anger. It was obvious that Len didn't relish being spoken to as "Ol' Man."

"From where to where is this drift fence goin' be built?" Len asked, voice suddenly hoarse.

Jim felt anger arising in him. This pair had plenty of brassy nerve to ride into his uncle's ranch, bold as daylight, after they had beaten him unconscious. He knew now, for sure, that this was the pair with whom he had fought. The bruise, livid and red, on the scar-face's neck told him that.

"You know me the next time you see me, 'puncher?" the scar-faced asked.

Jim nodded. "Which one of the Talbots are you?"

"Knife is the name. Why, an' who t'hell are you?"

He kept watching Jim, who said, "I'm Jim Rathburn."

"Kin to the old man here?" Knife wanted to know.

"His nephew."

Knife Talbot nodded, eyes puckered. Bowie Talbot looked at them, then swung his gaze back to Len.

"Where is this drift fence to go in?" Len Rathburn again demanded, knuckles white as he gripped the arms of his wheelchair.

"From the base of Black Saddle Butte across the range to them bluffs south of Sagehen Crick."

Jim heard his uncle's sudden intake of breath. He saw the wide nostrils of Broken Nose flare even wider. Knife Talbot, though, kept his eyes on him, and his eyes were narrowed even more.

"Acrost part of my range," Len Rathburn said.

Bowie Talbot shook his head slowly.

"Not your range, Rathburn. You have no deeds to that land; I have."

"I've run cattle there for six years."

"Yes, you have. But you ran on free range, government range. No legal deeds to the graze . . . I have the deeds."

"How did—you get them?"

"I bought out those farmers. By accident and luck, they took up homesteads in a row; I bought their deeds for a song. That whole bunch located over in that section sold out to me."

Len Rathburn wet his lips. "I don't believe that, Bowie Talbot! I don't think thet nester on Willer Crick will sell to you!"

"Which one you mean, Ol' Man?"

"None other than the father of that redheaded girl, name of Lester Jones. He told me he'd sell to nobody. Jes' last week he said that."

Bowie Talbot rocked his body in saddle. "You're right there. Lester Jones wouldn't sell to me. But there are ways to change a man's mind, you know. Ways to scare the jeepers out of him for once and for all. And, if he doesn't scare, you can always find a bullet that would like to meet him. . . ."

Jim listened. He remembered the pretty freckles that ran across the pert nose of Mary Jones. Now this redheaded girl was involved in this dark and terrible grass-war. That thought was not good.

Len Rathburn said angrily, "The Buckin' Horse outfit won't let you run thet drift fence, Talbot!"

Bowie Talbot smiled crookedly. "Us boys try to be good neighbours, Len. You won't let us work with you! We just want to warn you that if you ride against our bobwire, you'll regret the day!"

Bowied started to turn his horse. But Knife Talbot was still watching Jim. Bowie Talbot looked at his brother.

"Are you comin', or do you like this shirt-tail outfit so well you aim to bunk down here, Knife?"

Knife Talbot spoke from the corner of his mouth, words rapid. "I don't like the looks of this younger Rathburn, Bowie."

Bowie looked at Jim. Then he said

tonelessly, "He looks kinda harmless to me."

Jim spoke to Knife Talbot. "Howdy, *Casey*." Then his eyes went to Bowie Talbot. "An' how are you, *Casey?*"

The Talbots exchanged glances.

"Casey?" Knife Talbot demanded. "What the hell you talkin' about, Rathburn?"

"You forget fast, Talbot."

The knife scar stood out, a livid slash against the man's thin jowl. "You talk like a damned idiot. What am I supposed to remember?"

Jim said, "You two jumped me this morning. You got a mark along the base of your neck, Knife. That's where I hit you with a chair. You called each other Casey and you wore masks. *Where do you keep your masks when you're not usin' them?*"

Again, the brothers exchanged glances. This time it was Bowie Talbot who spoke. "So that's where you got that split lip and black eye. . . . You got us all wrong, Jim Rathburn. We're jes' a coupla Texas boys, loookin' for peace and prosperity on this Montana range. . . ."

"You might get prosperity," Jim replied angrily, "But you sure won't get peace, not after sluggin' me unconscious. Man to man, Knife Talbot, it's goin' to be you and me. Climb outa that saddle, Texas man, an' get some fists."

Knife answered the challenge by slipping his boot out of the stirrup and kicking viciously out, but Jim's reaction was a split second too quick and, as he ducked, he also grabbed for Knife's ankle and found it. With a twist and a heave he had Knife's leg over his shoulder and he heard his would-be assailant unloose an oath as he was dragged out of the saddle and hit the ground with a thud. It was then Jim heard somebody holler, "I got rifle on you, Bowie Talbot!"

For a moment, he did not recognize the voice, until he remembered the presence of the Squaw.

She stood in the doorway, a Winchester in her dark hands. And the black bore of the heavy .30-30 was on Bowie Talbot. A glance at Bowie showed his hands slowly rising, fear showing across his white face. A bullet, at such short range, would blow a hole in him the size of a man's fist!"

The squaw had been smarter than either Len and Broken Nose. A glance at the Sioux showed him standing with his hand on his gun. Len, Jim had noticed, had had a .45 holster attached to the side of his wheelchair. Now his uncle's right hand was on the gun's grip, but the gun was till in leather.

Quickly Jim turned his attention once more to his adversary for Knife, having made a cat-like recovery after hitting the ground, had pivoted round and had come up like a taut spring suddenly uncoiled. His eyes flashed with rage at the way Jim had handled him and he came in two-fisted for his revenge.

Jim promptly hit him in the mouth and he felt his knuckles skin as Knife grunted and fell back a pace before coming in again. This time his fists, big and hard-knuckled, were high up to protect his face, so that when Jim shot over a powerful left, Talbot took it on the forearm. Knife however was unable to find any counter for a cracking right which pierced his defence but he was still a rare handful, as Jim was soon to discover.

As both men weaved in and out trying to find a vulnerable spot Jim heard Len holler, "I've got my gun on you Bowie!" and knew there was no chance of the brothers ganging up on him as they had done in the hotel. It was just as well for at that moment he went down to a raking left hook that hit him full on the nose. He felt the spurt of blood and thought, "My nose always bleeds so easily. . . ."

He had to use all his cunning to keep away from Knife's rib-bustin' kicks but on his feet once again he began to swap punches with Knife, who, even if he knew little about the finer art of fistic science, was still tremendously strong and eager for the kill. Jim knew he had a fight on his hands right enough and the beating he had taken at the hotel wasn't helping his chances. His breath began to come painfully and, to conserve his strength, he ran into a clinch and caught the smell of saddle leather and blood. Although Knife had taken plenty he was never more dangerous than now and as they broke he swung a hay-maker that would have put Jim down again had he not sidestepped it.

Jim's ribs ached, a fist had broken open his lip again. He dug his head lower and the memory of the beating he had taken in the hotel room again surged over him. This rankled, and pride fired his muscles.

He hit out with a long and looping right that caught Knife Talbot on the side of the head. Jim missed with a left that followed, because already Talbot was going backwards, smashing into the hitch-rack, which brought him up sharply. Jim heard his shrill and painridden cry which suddenly shut off as he belted Talbot flush on the point. Talbot sagged, drooped forward, and the desperate fight was over. Jim stepped back, shirt hanging in ribbons from his belt, his body mauled and scratched, his breathing coming in short, agonized gasps.

"By golly, Jim boy, you did it!"

It was his uncle's jubilant voice.

Jim glanced at Broken Nose. For a moment, the hint of a smile played around the Sioux's stern lips, then this died and the great dark eyes became blank and fathomless. Jim looked at Squaw.

She stood in the doorway—big, stolid, heavy. With the Winchester still on Bowie Talbot.

Jim panted, words coming with an effort, "Thanks Squaw. You outguessed these—two would-be gunmen."

Jim looked at Bowie Talbot. The man's face was black with anger, the lips pulled down, the eyes slitted. Bowie Talbot looked at his unconscious brother.

"Throw a bucket of water on him," Bowie Talbot ordered tersely.

Len Rathburn turned to Broken Nose and said with sarcastic emphasis. "Go in and get some water and douse him. But make it hot water—boilin' hot."

The Sioux remained standing, impassive and his thoughts his own secret. Jim saw Squaw smile slowly and derisively.

Bowie Talbot answered, "Very funny Ol' Man," before turning to Jim with a cynical smile. "You knocked him out, it's your turn to bring him to. Give him a shot of water, Rathburn."

"That's more than you did for me in the hotel."

"They tell me," retorted Bowie, "that a pretty girl brought you out of it."

"You seem to know plenty about it, eh?" asked Jim.

"Not a thing, you can bet your sweet life about that," answered Bowie as he dismounted. He went to a trough and filled a bucket. He had an easy, liquid gait and, as he returned, bucket in hand, it was easy to see that he would dearly liked to have thrown the water over Jim, but the Squaw had her eyes on him, and he thought better of it when he saw that her dark hands still held the rifle.

"Sorry," Bowie murmured, and threw

the water into the face of his brother. Talbot stirred, got to his boots, and Bowie said sternly, "Get into leather and ride, you damned fool!"

"I'll finish him—"

Jim stood there, fists up. "You can have some more," he invited tonelessly.

Knife Talbot moved toward him, but his brother put out his arm and stopped him and said, almost quietly, "Not with fists, Knife . . . With a gun, later, fists settle nothing."

Knife spat blood, glared at Jim, then mounted slowly. Bowie swung up, looked at them, and cynicism was apparent in his words as he said, "It took four of you to whip one of us. . . ."

Then he whirled his bronc into the dust left by Knife Talbot's mount. The brothers slanted around the toe of the hill, and soon were out of sight. Only the sounds of hoofs, harsh and insistent against the Montana dry soil, came back to tell of their leaving.

Jim Rathburn spat blood. He looked at

his uncle and saw only a hollowness there, the traces of defeat.

"You acted fast, Jim. So fast I couldn't get my gun out of holster."

Jim said, "Think nothing of it, Len."

Broken Nose said, "We owe much to Squaw."

Sqauw looked at them. She was silent for a long moment, then she said, "The fists, they settle not a damn thing, like Bowie said. What did you gain by the fight, Jim?"

Jim Rathburn showed a battered grin. "Well, I won, for one thing."

"Victory no good," she scoffed. "What else you gain?"

"A damned tough enemy," Jim said quietly.

"The next time you two tangle," Len said dully, "it will not be with fists—it'll be with guns. . . ."

Jim nodded, face sombre. He had been on this Milk River range for less than twleve hours. The thought came that this would be Texas again—the Red River Wire Cutter's War.

And that thought was far from pleasant.

"It will be with guns," he agreed solemnly.

4

Short Gun Grass

REINS tied around the saddlehorn, the horse ran free, followed the dusty trail, hammer-head extended, and his steel-shod hoofs raising the dust, to show the progress of the two riders as they headed away from the Bucking Horse ranch.

The harsh voice of Bowie Talbot cut scornfully through the clatter of hoofs. "Hell of a fighter you turned out to be, Knife! Dang it, man, how many times have I told you not to use fists—use your boots, or your gun!"

Knife Talbot cocked his bloody head to one side, angry eyes taking in the form of his brother.

"Bowie, one more word out of you, and I'll drag you outa the saddle and beat you into the ground with my bare fists—"

"Like you hammered down Len Rathburn's nephew, eh, Knife?" Again, that naked, biting sarcasm.

Knife Talbot leaned back in the saddle, boots braced in oxbow stirrups. There was a sense of humour in him, although buried deep, and now it came to the surface, making a smile come to his knuckle-battered lips.

"Bowie, don't rub it in. I made a mistake. I aimed to kick him to sleep before he knew what had happened to him. But the boy is smart and fast—he upset my little ol' apple-cart. We maybe both didn't do so well by ridin' to the Buckin' Horse spread?"

"Why not? Explain that, Knife?"

"Well, we rode there to get ol' Len mad about this drift fence we're building, and to look over Jim Rathburn, to see how bad we had worked him over. We got ol' Len's goat, but we didn't do so well with Jim."

"You said a mouthful. That Texan is a tough bloke, Knife. His comin' here kinda changes the look of things. We had ol' Len where we wanted him . . . until he came along."

Bowie Talbot slowly unwrapped his latigo-leather bridle-reins from around the saddle-horn. He said, "Enough of this," and swung his bronc off the trail, heading toward the hills rimming the south border of Milk River Valley. The land was dry, and they rode past a farmer's wheat field where wheat had sprouted, grown about a foot high, and then died. There was not a bushel of wheat in the field of eighty acres.

"We got to get the titles to this land," Bowie said.

Knife Talbot replied, "We'll get them all. Martin Linklatter is on the cue-ball, he'll make money and we'll own the deeds in a few weeks. There's only that farmer on Willow Crick left. He hasn't signed over to Linklatter yet, but he will. This is no farmin' country."

"We've gone over that before."

"You don't sound too happy?"

Bowie Talbot snarled, "Don't talk like a fool. That Texan—that Jim Rathburn

—can handle a gun. Any man who is as fast with his dukes as he is, is also fast with a six-shooter."

His brother nodded. "Let's talk with this Lester Jones fellow," he said, swinging his bronc a little to the southeast.

"You sure it's him you wanna talk to, Knife?"

Knife Talbot turned dull eyes on his brother. "I don't foller you an inch, Bowie," he said, grinning widely.

"Well, what about Lester Jones's daughter, Mary. She was in the hotel and we didn't even know it. Anyhow she found Rathburn after we had worked him over. It was lucky we got out without her seeing us. She might have guessed who we were, even with the masks on. We must talk to her and find out if she suspects anything."

Knife grinned at his own thoughts. "I could run round in circles for that gal, Bowie," he volunteered. "She's got what it takes to make a man a contented man and then plenty to spare." Bowie shot his brother a quick glance.

They talked first with a farmer named White, who was taking down his barbwire fences. He was rolling the wire into loops and putting it in his wagon. He was a bowlegged man with a whiskery face that now sported a grin.

"The deed to my place will be in your hands in a few days, Bowie," he said. "My farmin' days are over. Now I kin go back to the saddle. How about a chance to git on the Heart Nine payroll as a ridin' man?"

Bowie shook his head.

Knife Talbot said, "We have to be careful. Right now quite a few people figure we deliberately hired you so-called *farmers* to squat on homesteads so we could buy your rights. If we put you to work for the Heart Nine, it wouldn't look good, White."

"Reckon not."

"We'll buy your bobwire an' posts though."

They dickered and at last agreed on a

price and White said he would deliver the barbwire and posts to the Heart Nine ranch, but Knife told him to unload the stuff three miles northeast on Sunken Coulee, where the drift fence would run across.

"Drift fence?" White's brows rose.

"Crew runnin' out in the mornin'," Knife Talbot said. "Bob wire an' posts going up from Black Saddle Butte plumb acrost to the bluffs along Sagehen Crick. Over ten miles of wire goin' in."

"Take gunsmoke to run it through, men."

"Mebbe so." Knife Talbot was non-committal. "So long, White, and thanks for the help." He reined his bronc around, stopped, said, "Seen Martin Linklatter today?"

"Druv by in his buggy about a hour ago."

The brothers exchanged glances before giving rein to their horses. They rode through sagebrush flats, and the smell was good, clean to their nostrils. They pounded across areas coated with greasewood, and because greasewood grew on the poorer soil, the hoofs of their broncs kicked up white alkali dust that hung like a cloud to mark their fast passing.

Each had his own private thoughts.

Bowie Talbot rode a pace behind his brother's mount, and he was thinking of a red-headed woman. This thought was pleasant, and this showed in the glistening of his eyes, for he wanted her. Knife Talbot was also thinking of a red-head. Not a woman, though, but a man who had beaten him unconscious, a red-headed fellow named Jim Rathburn.

There was, inside these two men, a deep sense of pride. Now the memory of the hard beating he had taken from Jim's fists flooded Knife Talbot, and it irked and tormented him. Word would get around that a Rathburn had fist-whipped a Talbot. It would become range gossip and an unbearable anger swept through him.

"I'll get him, Bowie."

"You'll get him," Bowie said, "or he'll get you. Very simple my beaten-up brother. You had a rep as a fist-fighter. You've whupped about six men on this range with your fists. But the knuckles of Jim Rathburn sure made you look like a novice."

"He got the jump on me. Next time, it will be different."

"I doubt it."

Knife looked at his brother, then decided he was "rawhiding" him. So he said, "Well, how about this farmer—this gent named Lester Jones?"

"Linklatter might have him seein' the light."

Knife nodded. "But what if he doesn't sell? He'll block thet drift fence all to hell. We can't go around him because of those cut-coulees behind his farm, and the land in front of him is gover'ment grass—and we sure ain't strong enough to run bobwire acrost land owned by Uncle Sam!"

"We'll make him sell!"

Knife said, "I don't cotton to pull guns against him."

"Because of Mary?" Bowie asked.

"Well, she's nice, an' she's purty—"

Bowie snarled, "Get her outa your mind, Knife! After this is over—after we own all of Milk River valley—then there'll be time for a woman. You go soft on me an' I'll run lead through you, brother or no brother!"

Knife's beaten face was flushed. "You talk like a locoed idiot, Bowie! Maybe I can use the girl. She's the apple of her ol' man's eye. Now, if I could convince her that her ol' man should sell—"

Bowie studied him. "You ain't got no influence with her," he said.

Knife lifted his wide shoulders, let them fall. "Jes' a thought," he said quietly.

Bowie Talbot only smiled. Their broncs fell to a fast trot, and within an hour, they were riding into the yard of the Jones' farm. The house, although small, was painted a white colour with green trim. Window boxes held geraniums and a wild morning glory covered the porch with its scarlet and blue flowers. Lester Jones, a bony and tall man of about fifty, came out of the brush-barn carrying two milk pails.

Bowie murmured, "Smoke from the chimney. Evidently the gal is home, mebbe gettin' breakfast. We got up early this mornin', Knife. . . ."

"You mean we didn't get to bed," his brother corrected.

Lester Jones stopped, said, "Howdy, Talbots."

"Howdy, Mr. Jones."

The air, for some reason, seemed suddenly tense. The Talbot brothers noticed immediately that Jones did not invite them to dismount, which was the first thing a man was asked to do when riding into a spread.

The barking of the collie had brought Mary to the door of the cabin. Both of the Talbots, upon seeing her, lifted their hats. The red-headed girl looked at Knife Talbot sharply, plainly surprised at the hammered condition of the cowman's face. She refrained from asking what had happened to him.

It was Knife himself who explained,

"Ran into the fists of Jim Rathburn, ol' Len's nephew. Rode over there peaceful like to talk to ol' Len an' this young one jumped me."

"What does Jim Rathburn look like?" Lester Jones enquired.

Bowie Talbot answered. "Bad as Knife looks. Claims somebody jumped him early this mawnin' in the hotel in town. Two men, he said, an' they looked like us, an' Knife tol' him, of course, he was loco an' then they had a set-to."

"My girl doctored young Jim Rathburn a bit, she told me."

"I never doctored him, as you say. I only was with him until the doctor came." Mary Jones looked at the Talbots. "Will you men have some coffee with us?"

"With pleasure," Knife said hurriedly, swinging down.

Bowie Talbot dismounted, noticing that Lester Jones was scowling. They trooped into the kitchen, spur rowels tinkling. Lester Jones followed and put the milk pails on the bench.

"Grab chairs, men, and fall to," he said.

Mary said, "I'll strain the milk, dad. I've already eaten."

Knife Talbot covertly watched the girl as he ate. She strained the milk through a cloth into milk pans and then carried the milk into the root cellar to cool. By this time the subject of conversation centred on the drift fence.

"Did you talk to Martin Linklatter, Jones?" Bowie Talbot asked, leaning back in his home-made chair.

"We talked." Lester Jones was abrupt.

"We offer you a good price," Knife Talbot said. "Two thousand dollars for the section of land you have here. That's over a buck and a half a acre, Jones."

"I won't sell."

The brothers exchanged quick, significant glances. To run the drift fence through they had to own the right to cross this strip of Willow Creek Range. Without it their scheme would be useless, for what was the good of a fence with a hole in the middle of it!

Knife Talbot's beaten face showed anger, but Bowie sent him a quick glance. "Well, that's every man's right, Mr. Jones," he said slowly. "But I do hope you get around to selling to us. I'll lay my cards on the table face up. We need your property or our drift fence will be worthless."

"My fences will block out Buckin' Horse cattle, men. And I promise no Buckin' Horse cows will cross through my gates to the east range."

Bowie shook his head.

"We can't run this on agreements. We run on deeds to land. We got to pertect ourselves. We got to get this Milk River range. The Buckin' Horse outfit has to go."

His words had a harsh finality and their purpose could not be mistaken.

Knife glanced at Mary. She nodded toward the door and went outside. Knife said, "Gotta go out an' look at my hoss's off-front hoof. Limped a little when I rode in." He turned to Jones. "You an' Bowie talk this over, eh?"

When Knife crossed the porch Mary was just entering a small log building, which her father used as a smithy. Knife followed her inside. He saw that her face was flushed and he could see the quick rise and fall of her bosom beneath the blouse she wore.

"You wanted to see me, Mary?" he asked.

"Yes, I did, Knife."

He moved closer to her and she stood still although she seemed excited. She caught the harsh odour of tobacco and leather gear—the male odour of a saddleman.

"What do we talk about, Mary?"

She looked at him for a moment before replying. "Dad is stubborn," she explained, "He might not sell to you boys."

Knife stared at her. He wanted her badly and the thought came to him that she had been in his mind for a long time. He didn't want to scare her so he replied, "I know he's stubborn, Mary."

"What . . . if he doesn't sell, Knife?"

The girl looked up at him as she spoke. Knife could see the faint trace of freckles across her flushed, piquant face. Her presence excited him, but he answered quietly enough, "We gotta git this range."

"And if Dad won't sell," she persisted.

"We'll get this grass even if it means guns."

Mary nodded as if she understood. She had still to play her best card. "But how about me?" she asked. "What if I get killed, Knife? Is the grass worth so much to you that you would endanger my life, too?"

He put an arm round her and she stiffened but forced herself to move closer to him.

"I could love you plenty, woman," he said as he pressed close to her.

She braced her hands against him and pushed herself free. "You haven't answered my question. In any case we must go now otherwise Dad and your brother might become suspicious."

They got outside as Bowie and Lester

Jones came out of the house. Nothing further passed between Knife and the girl.

Knife and Bowie Talbot mounted. Bowie kept his voice under rigid control. "You might change your mind, Jones. Whenever you want to peddle go and see Linklatter. He's our agent in this matter."

"I won't sell. I've developed this place. It ain't payin' off now because of the drought, but next year it might. When I saw this spread, I said to Mary, 'This is the end of the trail for your father. When he dies he dies on this land and is buried here.'"

Bowie nodded, watching Mary, who was looking at her father. Maybe Knife was right; maybe this girl could be utilized; maybe her influence would change this stubborn farmer's mind. . . .

Bowie answered, "A nice thought."

There was no use for further talk, so the Talbots swung their mounts around and loped away. They headed for town with Bowie Talbot riding a pace in the lead with his thick face scowling.

Suddenly Bowie turned in saddle and looked at his brother. "You have any luck, Romeo?"

"What do you mean?"

"Lay off the bluffin', Knife. You an' that gal talked in the blacksmith shop. Hardly big enough to hold two people unless they're mighty close together. . . ." Implication was heavy in his sultry voice. "What did she do, and say?"

"Said she'd work on her father for us."

Bowie smiled, eyebrows tilted. "That *all* that happened?"

Knife grinned. "That's all, my lovin' brother." He squinted at the rider ahead who was loping towards them, dust lifting behind his bronc. "Ain't that Smoky Ames, our hoss jingler?"

"Sure is. Ridin' fit to kill Heart Nine hossflesh, too."

Smoky Ames was a young fellow—slender and wiry. He pulled in and more dust rose and through it came his words.

"Been lookin' for you two. This Len Rathburn—he's got a nephew on this grass—he had a fight down town this mawnin'—"

Bowie snapped, "We know about it! That all you got to say, kid?"

"Not all of it, Bowie. Joe Matthews an' Jake Smith was ridin' south range this mornin'. They's a herd of cattle comin' up from the south, about five thousand head or so, they figured."

"Cattle!" exclaimed Knife.

"Who owns them?" Bowie Talbot demanded.

"They got the Buckin' Hoss iron on them," Smoky Ames panted. "They belong to this nephew—this Jim Rathburn!"

The brothers exchanged glances and Knife Talbot said slowly, "Five thousand head—and cattle short of feed as it is on Milk River. . . . Hell, a herd that size will wipe out what little surplus winter feed there is on the ground, Bowie!"

"They won't winter on Milk River," Bowie Talbot snarled.

5

Longhorns North

JIM RATHBURN washed his face in the horsetrough and wiped gingerly on a towel given him by Squaw. He grinned with effort and said, "Hope my mug doesn't look as bad as it feels."

Squaw said, "Looks worse maybe. . . ." She took the towel and waddled toward the house with Jim and Broken Nose and Len following in the wheelchair.

Once in the house Squaw said, "We have enough of fightin'. Now we all eat."

She set a bountiful table. Bacon fried just right, creamy hotcakes and fluffy biscuits. Jim was surprised to find genuine butter on the table. Usually the cowmen just used lard for butter, because lard was easy to buy, coming in five gallon pails.

"You keep a milk cow, Len?" Jim asked, winking at Broken Nose.

Len sputterd, "Milk cow—? Man, they'll never be no milk cow on this spread—biggest nuisance a man can have—can't stay away over night. This butter was made by the nester girl, Mary Jones."

"Thought you were mad at the farmers?" Jim asked.

"Hard to git mad at her, Jim."

Jim said, "That sure is the truth." His meal finished, he pushed back his chair, the legs grating on the floor. "This Texas son has to hit the trail south to his herd. How about loanin' me a hoss?"

"Barn full of 'em, Jim. Only wish I could ride with you—"

"When you get sense enough not to ride into an ambush, then you can ride range with me—but not before, Len," Jim joked, getting to his feet. "Thanks, Squaw." He added, "That meal reminded me of my mother's cooking."

"You eat many of my meals, Jim."

Jim grinned. "Hope you're right!" He

went outside and Broken Nose followed, loosening his gunbelt to accommodate for his big breakfast. "Where you goin', Broken Nose?"

"Me? I ride with you, Jim."

"You ain't on my payroll. If you was you'd be workin' for jawbone. No, you're workin' for Len, not for me."

"I ride with you, then."

"How come you wanna ride with me?"

"Len, he tell me to, Jim."

Jim smiled as he ran his eyes over the horses tied in the stalls. Although the interior of the barn was rather dark he could still see that the Bucking Horse iron had really good stock. Long-legged broncs with a dash of hot blood in them to give them speed and agility. Yet, mixed with this trace of thoroughbred blood, was the strain of local range horses—horses that could stand the grind of exhausting round-up circling, of rough slants that raised trouble with a bronc's foreshoulders. Jim selected a lanky sorrel gelding and led him out for saddling.

"I'm old enough to take care of myself,

Broken Nose. Shucks, I even voted in the elections down in Texas."

"Your uncle he so order."

Jim flattened his Navajo saddle-blanket on the sorrel's back. He was sort of glad the Sioux was riding with him. This was troubled range, he had had enough proof of that during the last few hours, and it was good to have a gun-pal riding by his stirrup. He completed his preparations, but suddenly the sorrel humped his back until a touch on the ribs restored him to good humour once more.

Broken Nose had thrown his Denver saddle over a stout black gelding. "Me ready to ride, Jim," he said.

They thundered out of the yard. Len had wheeled his chair out on the porch and he lifted a hand to them as they slanted across the compound. Then their hoofs rang against the planks of the bridge and they were out of sight in the high cottonwood trees whose leaves were coated by dust.

Jim took the lead, feeling the strength of his fresh bronc. The sorrel ran with his head down, and his gait was easy. He glanced at Broken Nose. The black was a hard-riding horse, but the Sioux sat his saddle like he had been glued onto it.

Jim hollered, "Good range, Indian."

"If it rain soon," the Sioux said. "If no rain then the cattle they die this winter. . . ."

Twisting in the saddle Jim turned to his companion once more and asked, "Good hoss country?"

The Sioux nodded. "Hoss not worth anything, not pay to be railed. Hoss live in snow like buffalo."

Jim sent his glance toward the north. There, beyond Milk River, rose the low hills, lifting up to become benchlands. They ran north and then became part of Canada. For a moment, then, a vague regret hit the young cowman. Because of barbwire, he had to leave his native land, going into Canada with his herds. But the Canadians, he knew, were good people, and there was range there. . . .

At this point, Milk River valley was about seven miles wide, with the town of

Branding Iron now a little to the east, smuggled in the cottonwoods on a little plateau that overlooked Milk River, which made a bend at this point. He looked at the southern rim of the valley. Here the hills lifted suddenly, with only one or two places where a man on horseback could climb onto the benchland.

He looked at Broken Nose. "Where do we bring down cattle, Sioux?"

The dark thick hand lifted and the forefinger pointed at the high cliff directly south. "Trail come down there. Narrow trail, though. Only one cow she walk alone, it that narrow."

Jim looked at the hills. At first, because of the distance, he could not see the trail; then, he saw it—a grey ribbon, thin against the rising heat of the day, that twisted upward through sandstone rocks, and skirted a few deep coulees. If a steer slipped off that trail, it would be lucky to escape death.

"My cows are leg weary," he said.

"We take them slow. When do we get to the rimrock trail, Jim?"

"Tomorrow. We're about fifteen miles south, I figure. The boys will be movin' them along, waitin' for me."

"Rider ahead, Jim."

The rider turned out to be nobody else than Mary Jones. Jim admired her red hair as it peeped out from under her Stetson. He could see the freckles on her saucy, turned-up nose.

"Hello, honey," he said.

She ignored him. "Howdy, Broken Nose."

Broken Nose said, "You know Jim?"

"Oh, yes," she said. "I've met him."

Jim grinned. "Two red-heads, you and I, and both hot-headed," he said to the girl. "Do I look any worse than I did a few hours ago?"

"Worse," she said. "I'll bet Knife Talbot beat you up good."

"Who told you?" Jim wanted to know.

She explained about the Talbots visiting her father. She also mentioned the drift fence and said that it would cause trouble. Her father, she said, would not sell his place.

"You ever talk to Len about sellin'?" Jim asked.

"He won't sell to Len Rathburn—and he won't sell to the Heart Nine, either."

Jim said nothing. Plainly the girl was worried. She had reason to be. She and her father were sitting in the middle of a pond and the buckbrush bristled and glistened with rifles. The Talbots were not men to trifle with. Never for one moment did Jim Rathburn underestimate the power and ruthlessness of the Heart Nine owners. They had demonstrated their viciousness in the attack at the hotel, and later when they had openly and brazenly ridden to Len's ranch where he and Knife had tangled to some purpose.

Broken Nose asked, "Where the Talbots ride to, girl?"

"They headed for Branding Iron."

Broken Nose looked at Jim. "We have to ride through town," the Sioux said.

Jim grinned. "I'm not afraid of 'em," he said. He looked impishly at Mary Jones. "Ride right close to me, honey."

"Oh, yeah . . . I suppose you want me

to climb right in the saddle with you, Texas man?"

"That sure would be nice," Jim said quickly. "I could hold you an' lead your bronc. Why not do that?"

She blushed. Her freckles stood out even more. "Some other time," she said. "Let's make tracks. I'm heading into town for our mail. Stage comes in today."

She rode a chunky horse, not much more than a pony, which despite being short-legged, had rare speed. She could ride, too. The wind took off her hat, so that it hung from her neck by the throat-strap, her red hair glistened in the sun. The wind pushed her shirt against her revealing graceful contours.

For the time being, at least, Jim forgot the trouble that hung like a dark cloud over the Milk River country as he contemplated the possibility of getting Miss Mary Jones, curves, freckles and all, into his arms. She wasn't the first young woman he had met by any means, or had had similar thoughts about, and he wondered what his chances were with her. He had to admit to himself that he didn't rate them very highly.

When they reached Branding Iron, they slowed to a walk, the girl riding between Jim and Broken Nose.

"Well, here's where I leave you, men."

Jim said, "Hope you get a letter from your boy friend, honey."

"I have no such friend."

Jim chuckled. "I was only devilin' you," he explained, "but it's nice to know that I have the field all to myself!"

"Quite the romantic, aren't you?" replied Mary with heavy sarcasm.

She rode over to the post-office and dismounted. Jim took in the pioneer cowtown at a glance. Evidently the mail had just come in, for the stage was halted in front of a livery barn, where a hostler was busy unhooking the foam-flecked team. A couple of saddlehorses were tied to the rack in front of the town store and Jim recognised them as the broncs belonging to the Talbots.

It was just at that moment that a man, yet another stranger to Jim, stepped out of the Broken Cinch saloon, looked at Jim and yelled, "Rathburn, I'm comin' at you!"

Jim turned in the saddle, staring at his challenger. He was a hulking, long-armed individual of about fifty, with thick jowls, covered by black whisker-stubble. He moved to the edge of the plank sidewalk and crouched with both hands resting on the black handles of his two holstered .45s.

"Comin' at you, Rathburn!" the man snarled again, deep in his gunman's crouch.

Jim felt a moment of indecision. He didn't know who his challenger was but the man knew him right enough. It was then that Jim realised suddenly that the affair had been specially got up for his benefit. No doubt the Talbots were behind it. The gunman for a certainty would be one of their hired hands and he had been given a job of work to do—the quick and total elimination of Jim Rathburn. It stuck out a mile.

Jim replied, "Hell, I don't know you

from Adam, mister. Why do you want trouble with me?"

Already a crowd was beginning to collect and down by the livery barn the hostler stopped unhooking the stage team and stood, silent and rigid, watching through wide eyes.

The gunman snarled, "You don't know me! Like hell you don't! You know me danged well enough! You done me plenty dirt down in Texas! Now I'm a' goin' to make you pay, you lyin', double-crossin' rat!"

Jim repeated, "I don't know you."

The man moved off the sidewalk three paces, boots scuffling dust. His eyes never left Jim. Then he stopped again—a compact hunk of muscle, tense and ready for action.

"Tell that to the marines!" he jeered. "How come you get thet herd of cattle you're drivin' in on this range?" He answered his own question. "You an' me robbed a Texas bank. That's how you got the dinero to buy them cows."

Jim never let his gaze leave the

gunman. From the corner of his mouth he spoke to Broken Nose.

"This is a trap. Who is this guy?"

"Never seen him before."

Jim nodded, said, "Watch the Talbots . . . They jus' come out of thet store. This gent works for them, or else I'm loco." He looked at the gunman. "I never saw you before in my life!"

The man began to curse him in bar-room language.

"You ran out on me durin' that holdup. You grabbed the money and I went to jail. But I broke out and I trailed you, Rathburn. Fill your hand, you coward!"

Then, without further warning, the man's guns began to lift.

6

When Killers Meet

STILL in the saddle, sitting a quiet horse, Jim drew his left hand gun, for his right hand still held the bridle reins. He heard a woman scream a warning, and he thought it came from Mary Jones. He heard the scuffle of shoe leather as men and women darted away to safety from the bullets that threatened.

Then, all these sounds, became lost in the roar of gunfire. Jim felt the fork of his saddle move under savage impact. He realised his assailant had opened up and one of his bullets, thrown in haste, had ploughed into the fork of the Amarillo hull.

Jim remembered his own gun coming up, remembered it bucking against the palm of his hand—spitting its deadly, hot death. He remembered how the bullets hit the stranger in the chest so that he began to stumble. He did not hate this man, even if he was low enough to kill for a few lousy dollars.

The man screamed, head back and the cords of his thick neck straining. Jim saw him drop his guns, saw dust lift as the heavy Colts thudded down. Then, arms at his side, the man lurched ahead, dead on his feet. He hit the tie-rack, slid along it, and fell on his side.

Only then did Jim let the air escape his tight lungs. Anger flooded over him like a tide and he felt stifled with rage. The Talbots, he saw, had taken a few paces forward and they stood looking at the body of the dead gunman—the hired assassin who was to have gunned Rathburn out of his saddle and thus removed a rival they had so far been unable to dispose of.

Jim said to the Sioux, "Swing your six-shooters round and cover the Talbots."

"There's two of them, don't forget," answered Broken Nose.

"Two of us, too."

He dismounted, glancing at the rip where a bullet had ploughed into the fork of the saddle, Jim felt his boots hit the dust and he walked towards Knife and Bowie who stood vigilant and tensed with their hands on their guns. They awaited him, keen-eyed and hard, and as wary as foxes. A crowd of spectators, sensing yet more trouble, stood silent and expectant.

Bowie looked beyond him, saw the gun in the dark thick hand of Broken Nose, the Sioux, and Jim heard the cowman murmur, "The Injun has a gun on us, Knife. . . ."

"I can see it!"

Jim stopped. Gun still in hand, he looked at Knife Talbot. Hate for him glistened in the rider's beady eyes, in the set of the swollen face.

"Do you know that gunman, Knife?"

Knife Talbot's tongue came out and wet his lips. "Never saw him afore in my life. He knew you."

"He lied, and you lie!"

Agger flushed the Texan's face, giving

him a tough appearance. Jim swung his eyes to Bowie Talbot who eyed him with a sort of cynical glance.

"Do you know him, Bowie?"

"Never seen him before in my life. But, like Knife said, he seemed to know you —Trailed you up from the Lone Star state to kill you—"

"He lied. And you lie. Your money is in his pocket right now—"

"Don't call me a hired—"

Jim clipped down with his .45. The blow was quick and unexpected. The barrel of his heavy .45 knocked off Bowie's stetson as it came rocking down against the man's forehead.

The hat spun into the dust. Bowie Talbot folded to his knees, blood running across his face. Jim slugged him again and knocked him full length on the plank sidewalk, where he lay still. Jim swung his gun again, but Knife Talbot ducked, moving quickly backward.

"Rathburn, I'll kill you. So help me, I'll kill you. You got that Injun with a gun on me—"

Jim spoke to Broken Nose. "Drop your sights off him, Sioux." He did not look at the man. But he heard the Sioux say, "I holster my gun, Jim."

Jim put his .45 back into leather. He said coldly, "All right, Knife Talbot, pull your cutter!"

Knife Talbot, his eyes bright and gleaming, flickered his hands down to his holstered guns in a movement that resembled forked lightning. Jim was in the act of drawing when between them, unexpectedly came a man. Jim caught his draw in time, otherwise he would have shot the intruder. Talbot also was prevented from shooting, for the man had grabbed him around the middle, pinning his arms to his sides.

"Let go of me, Harden—"

Jim caught a glimpse of shiny steel on the man's vest, and he remembered his uncle mentioning the name of the sheriff.

Harden panted, "Help me, somebody—"

Two townsmen moved in, pinning

Knife Talbot against the wall. Knife Talbot suddenly stopped struggling, his eyes riveted on Jim Rathburn.

"I'll be all right," he said quietly.

One man looked inquiringly at Sheriff Harden. The lawman nodded and the townsmen stepped back, leaving Knife Talbot standing against the wall, only his eyes alive in his hate-filled face.

Broken Nose said, "Me, my gun is up again, Jim."

Jim nodded, not looking at the Sioux. His gaze was on Sheriff Harden. A tall thin man, this badge-toter, his face fascinated Jim. It was terribly pale and was the visage of a very sick man. Yet, his strength had been formidable in pinning the arms of Knife Talbot.

Harden's dark eyes, sunken and surrounded by dark rings, touched Jim, and Jim saw the man's thin lips move.

"Rathburn, get out of town!"

"I run from no man!"

The eyes turned into black steel. "You

heard me. Get out of town. I'll talk with you later about this—and about the affair at the hotel this morning. Beat it now, or go to jail!"

Anger still rode Jim Rathburn. He looked at the dead gunman. He looked at Bowie Talbot, who was sitting up, head in his hands. His eyes met those of Knife Talbot.

"Try to run me out, sheriff."

Broken Nose said, "Jim, do as Harden he say."

Jim turned and looked at the Sioux. Anger left him then and he said, "Sorry, sheriff," and he went into leather. He looked at Mary Jones, who was among a little group of spectators. He lifted his hat, once again his own self, and said, "I'm sorry you had to see that, Miss Jones."

She did not reply.

Jim and Broken Nose rode down the street, both silent. Tension was leaving Jim, allowing him to relax, to think clearly. A man had come out of a small log building. On the window of the building Jim read the sign:

Martin Linklatter
Land Locator U.S. Land Office
Farmers, see me—I'll locate you on good land!

He was a heavy-set man of about forty, with a beefy face now marred by a cigar stuck between fat lips. His gaze met that of Jim. For a moment they studied each other.

Jim reined in close to the sidewalk. The man stared at him, cigar rigid.

Jim said, "So you're the gent that swindles the farmers, eh?"

"I don't understand you," Linklatter said, talking around the cigar.

"I have an idea that you do."

"You're barking up the wrong tree, mister."

"Rathburn is the name. Jim Rathburn."

"I know it. Word gets around fast in this small town. But I figure you're still on the wrong side of this fence, Rathburn."

"You're figurin' counts for nothin'!"

"Cattlemen are doomed. They can't operate without free range and certainly not in this country."

"You're not workin' for the farmers. You work for the Talbots!"

Linklatter took the cigar from his thick lips and turned it slowly between steady fingers. He seemed absorbed in the operation until finally he lifted his eyes.

"Rathburn," he said, "You talk tough, and some day somebody will have to kill you. . . ."

For answer Jim spat in his face.

Martin Linklatter didn't move. He only looked at Jim but his eyes were alive. They reflected the lust to kill.

"That *somebody* might be me," he said, voice harsh.

"When you feel lucky, have a go," challenged Jim.

Linklatter had a grip on himself. "Time will tell," he answered.

He turned, stalked into his office. Jim

whirled his bronc and loped out of Branding Iron, with Broken Nose riding at his side.

"You make enemy, Jim."

"That's all right with me, Broken Nose."

7

Six-gun Strategy

NEW Justin boots, highly polished, rested on the desk. Sunlight came through the window to reflect their shiny black surfaces.

Land Locator Martin Linklatter leaned back in his swivelchair, the spring creaking, as he studied his new boots.

Knife Talbot, squatting with his back against the wall, also looked at the boots, as his brother crossed and recrossed the small office. Finally the movement was too much for his nerves and Knife snarled, "Sit down, for hell's sake, Bowie! You're drivin' me loco!"

Bowie stopped and looked down at his brother. "Your nerves are as raw as if a rasp had run over them. When you talk to me, talk in a gentler voice, savvy?"

"I'll talk to you as I see fit!"

They glared at each other. Two brothers fired by the same greed, banded together not because the same blood tumbled through their veins, but because greed motivated them both, and two men had a better chance to get Milk River valley than had one.

Linklatter said, "Take it easy, you two gun wolves . . ." and his tone was placating.

As Bowie spread his legs wide with spurs jangling his brother ran the tip of his finger along the deep bitten scar that scored his jowl. Their glances met and they regarded each other with ill-disguised antagonism.

Then, for some reason, Bowie Talbot smiled. He felt his damp hair and grinned again.

"Buffaloed me down like I was a town drunk. Damn, he's fast with his gun. There I stood, sound asleep, figurin' he'd fire, not buffalo! Doc sure made me howl when he put them stitches in my scalp!" He looked at his fists. "But I'll make thet nephew of ol' Len's howl when I tangle with him next."

"He made you look bad," Linklatter said slowly. "The whole town saw you hit the dust, Bowie. You once had a rep as a tough gent . . . but I doubt if it holds good now."

"You didn't do much! He hocked spit right into your homely mug an' you stood there an' took it!"

Linklatter looked at him, and made a steeple out of his fingers. In this way he hid his anger . . . and his fear.

"Harden had to shove in his bill," Knife Talbot murmured. "Else I'd've finished off this Red River bucko."

"Maybe," Bowie Talbot scoffed. "Maybe!"

"Don't rub my hide the wrong way, Bowie. Don't push your brother, Bowie, 'cause he don't want no trouble with his blood kin. . . ."

Linklatter let his boots fall to the floor. He leaned forward, face earnest, and he said, "Men, if we fight among ourselves, we sure can't whip the Buckin' Horse outfit. What did Lester Jones say?"

"He won't sell," Knife Talbot murmured, still fingering his scar. "We talked to him before we rode into town."

Linklatter looked at Bowie Talbot, and his brows rose. Bowie said, "A dose of fire. Maybe some hot lead. We'll do the job tonight."

Knife looked at his brother, said, "Thought we were to jump this Texan's herd tonight? We can't be in two places at once."

"Tomorrow night, we can jump the cattle. It will be easier then. The herd will bed down on Tanner's Wash and tomorrow night will suit as well as any time."

Knife Talbot said, "I don't want thet girl hurt."

Bowie turned on his brother, staring at him. "You've gone for her, eh?"

Knife Talbot got to his feet and moved forward, fists up. He said, "Bowie, watch your dirty tongue," and then Linklatter moved his bulk between them. He got them apart and when he stepped back he was panting.

Bowie Talbot stopped, breathing a little too hard, and then his humour broke through, making him smile, "Sorry, Knife."

Knife Talbot watched his brother and finally said, "Sorry, Bowie." To Linklatter he remarked, "You've got strength. More than I figured you would have, sittin' aroun' as you do. . . ."

Linklatter sat down, looked at his boots. "All right, we only have one obstacle, and that is this Jones farmer."

"Where are the deeds? Did they come on the stage?" Bowie Talbot asked the question.

Linklatter opened a drawer and said, "These came today. All legal and from the land office in Helena. Six of them there. Letter said the others would come on the next stage. A little slow in filing them down there."

"Come mornin'," Bowie Talbot said, "we run out the wagons with posts and bobwire. Our cowpunchers will be diggin' post holes tomorrow."

Linklatter nodded, said, "All right. We ride tonight, eh? Where do I meet you? Same line cabin?"

Bowie said, "Sunken Springs line camp. Be there at nine. By the time we get from there to the Jones' farm it will be late and dark enough."

They trooped out, dusty riders, men of the rope and gun and saddle. Martin Linklatter watched them go into the store to finish buying barbwire and fencing supplies. The land locator rubbed his jaw. Fear was in him.

He remembered Jim Rathburn riding close to the sidewalk and looking at him. He remembered the steely glances the Red River man had given him and the way he had talked.

Before this range war was over, somebody would be killed. Martin Linklatter filled his lungs full of good air. He wanted to keep on breathing. But he couldn't forget Jim Rathburn.

The land locator went outside. He

moved down the street, nodding to people; they did not seem as cordial as usual. He realised that he, too, had lost face; Jim Rathburn had taunted him, had deliberately spat in his face. The memory of it stirred his anger afresh.

Someone said, "Can I talk to you a minute, Linklatter?"

He turned, annoyance scrawled on his face. Across the street, Knife Talbot was tying a pair of framepliers onto his saddle. The Heart Nine man heard the sheriff call to Linklatter, and he turned and watched with interest. And he heard every word that was said.

"Somethin' I can do for you, Sheriff Harden?"

The lawman nodded. "This Rathburn gent—he spat in your face. You could file a warrant for his arrest and I'll serve it."

"What would be the charge?"

"Disturbin' the peace, for one."

Linklatter opened his mouth to speak, but before he could utter a word a man, standing close by, said, "Or it could be *spittin' in the face of a coyote!*"

Linklatter turned, looked at the man, and said, "I'll come over there and beat in your face, Clinton!"

"Come ahead, you no good chiselin' land locator."

The sheriff said, "Clinton, that's enough."

Clinton said, smiling, "Rathburn gave him enough—and gave it to him pronto. What you goin' to do about it, land locator?"

"When I see him again, I'll kill him!"

Clinton said, "Talk is cheap but it takes money to buy bullets." He went down the street. He ran a few head of cattle back in the brakes. He did not like Linklatter because the man had taken in farmers.

Linklatter said, "I'll handle this my way, sheriff. No warrant, thanks."

He turned and went to his office. Suddenly he hated this town and these people, the whole stinking set-up. He went to the wall safe and twirled the dial. He looked at the currency and bills in the safe. They had paid him well, the dumb farmers and the Talbots.

He stood there, deep in thought. At that moment the Talbots rode by at a walk, heading for the Heart Nine. Knife Talbot looked and saw him standing there outlined in the window.

Knife said, "Was that safe door open, Bowie?"

"Looked to me like it was." Bowie Talbot studied his brother. "Why?"

"Are you sure you know the combination?"

"Yes. I saw Linklatter open it one day. He thought he was shielding the dial from me but I looked around him."

Bowie Talbot intoned some figures, mentally opening the safe. Then he realised that Knife was not listening. His brother's seamed face had a long and thoughtful look.

"What's the deal?"

"Linklatter might try to run. He might have been countin' his dough. He's run his string to the end of the line here. He knows it. He talked with Sheriff Harden. Clinton egged him on and Linklatter, for once, lost his head."

"What did he say?"

"He threatened to kill Jim Rathburn."

Bowie Talbot nodded, mind busy. "You got something there. We could get rid of Linklatter, recover our money and that spent by the farmers, and still lay the blame on Jim Rathburn, eh?"

"Everybody heard him threaten to kill Jim Rathburn. Word could get to Rathburn. Rathburn *could* gun down Linklatter."

"How could we lay the blame on Rathburn?" Bowie asked.

His brother scowled and spat tobacco juice. "If only we had somethin' to leave on Linklatter's carcass—somethin' that belongs to Rathburn and would fix the blame."

"I got it," Bowie suddenly said.

Knife smiled wryly. "My Gawd," he commented, "however did an idea light into that thick skull of yours? What's the shatterin' scheme, Bowie?"

Bowie pounded his fist on the fork of his saddle. "Remember when we were over at the Buckin' Horse spread this mornin'?" His brother nodded and Bowie went on, "Well, did you see the suitcase Jim Rathburn had taken over there? It was sittin' on the end of the porch."

Knife nodded, eyes small and thoughtful. "He must have brought the case over from the hotel. I remember seein' it there. Wonder what's in it?"

"There must be something in it which could be left as a bit of evidence."

"Good idea, Bowie. Come dark, you sneak over to the Buckin' Horse, try to get into that suitcase. Shouldn't be hard. Squaw hits the hay early and ol' Len ain't no count on thet wheel chair."

"I'll do that. Then I meet you an' Linklatter at Sunken Springs, eh? Then we ride to the Jones' outift. . . ."

Knife said, "That Mary Jones—she's makin' a fool outa me. She's a smart wench. Plays along with me just to find out what she can, and all the time she laughs at me up her sleeve."

"You jes' find that out?" Bowie Talbot asked. "She tried it on me but she never got nowhere. Come on, hit the dust, cowboy."

They loped towards the Heart Nine outfit.

8

Trailherd

JIM and Broken Nose had left Branding Iron town two miles behind when they heard the rattle of hoofs behind them. They were jogging along easily, talking about the run-in with the Talbots and Linklatter when Jim caught the approach of another rider and turned in his saddle, wondering if it might not be Sheriff Harden with a warrant. It wasn't. The rider had red hair and was much prettier than Harden.

"Miss Mary, again." Jim smiled widely. "The Jones farm, though, is to the north of Brandin' Iron, and this direction is straight south."

Broken Nose grinned, then winked at Jim. "This girl she liked you, Jim."

Mary heard his remark. "This is no time for joking," she said. "Linklatter was asked by Sheriff Harden if he wanted to sign a warrant for your arrest, Jim. Linklatter said no. Then one of the little cowmen back in the hills, a fellow named Clinton, threw some jibes into Linklatter, and he lost his head. He said he'd kill you, Jim."

"Thanks for callin' me Jim. Up to now, it's been Mr. Rathburn, I believe."

She looked at him in surprise. "Aren't you—well, sorta worried, *Mr. Rathburn?*"

Jim idly whirled his quirt. "I figured he'd aim to get me anyway, without him makin' a public statement. That makes three of them now—the two Talbot skunks and this land locator. Wonder who thet gent was that I had to kill? Anybody know his name?"

Apparently nobody in town knew the man. He had hung around the saloons for a few days and had offered to hire out his gun to anybody who wanted a fast gun. But apparently nobody had seen him talking to either of the Talbot brothers.

The fix-up had evidently been carried out with the utmost secrecy.

"Harden isn't mad about you killing him," Mary said. "That was self defence." For a moment her face became stormy. "This is really dangerous range and I fear for my father."

Jim said, "He should play in with the Talbots. This ain't no farmin' country. Too dry and the soil is bad."

"He's—he's stubborn."

They rode along, the sun slanting down. The air had become chilly. The sudden change made Jim think of blizzards down on the Red River. One moment the sky would be clear and the sun warm and then the wind would start to howl and sleet would fall.

"I've never seen men working a trail herd," Mary said.

Jim said, "I can take a hint. All right, we got an extra bedroll, and you can have the bedwagon to yourself. But I warn you about one thing, and I'm serious."

She looked at him in surprise. "And what's that, Jim?"

"My boys haven't seen a woman for weeks now, and I dare say some of them never saw a girl as purty as you, Miss Mary. So if you get hugged and kissed, jes' remember it tain't my fault."

"Oh, shucks, quit joking!"

"You know something?"

"What?"

"We've known each other for all of twelve or so hours and we've only had about six spats during that time. We should get married."

She looked at Broken Nose. "Does he propose to all his women in such a short time, Broken Nose?"

"Me no know him long, Miss Mary."

Mary said, "Well, it's nice to have a sense of humour. It isn't everybody that can joke with a pistol stuck in his back. Say, is winter coming?"

They were climbing out of Milk River valley, following the rimrock trail. The wind was gathering in intensity and it was steadily becoming colder. It was blowing in from the northwest down from the far-distant Canadian Rockies. When they rode behind the huge sandstone boulders the wind was less keen, but the sun was still thin and without warmth. Days were short at this time of the year this far to the north east. The sun already was due to go down.

Again, Jim Rathbrun felt a vague feeling of unrest. He had intended to winter his herd in Milk River valley. He had expected his uncle to have a surplus of hay in the corrals, but such was not the case—drought had made the hay crop small.

The valley was overstocked with cattle and he was facing a dangerous predicament. He had to get his herd through the winter ahead. To do so he had to feed the cattle hay or get on a range where grass was long and the cattle could rustle in the open. Of course there was always fodder to be bought. He could freight it in on bobsleds at a pinch, but what was he to use for money?

His crew had not been paid since he left the Red River country. Jim reckoned he must have about two hundred dollars left, but this would be needed to keep himself and the crew going. Canada seemed to be the answer to his problems, but to get there a late winter was needed, and all the signs showed there was no prospect of this happening. In fact, everything appeared to be going wrong and an early fall of snow would leave no choice but to winter on Milk River.

As if he had read Jim's thoughts Broken Nose said, "Winter come very early some years."

Jim grunted. "An' I suppose this will be one of those years. Jes' my luck. Well, anyhow let's make tracks, riders."

They had reached the summit. To the south ran the rolling hills and the benchlands. Buffalo grass, dried and short, was already being covered with snow, and the wind that drifted it in was raw and cold.

Mary had her long sheepskin coat tied behind her saddle and Jim helped her put it on, leaning from the saddle as he did so. She found a pair of warm mittens in the pockets of the garment.

"You can never tell about the weather

in Montana," she told Jim. "You got to be prepared for a blizzard on the Fourth of July, they tell me."

"Almost as bad as Texas," Jim grunted. "My overcoat is in the bed wagon. How cold will it get, Broken Nose?"

"Not too cold. Snow maybe, then it melt. Too early for winter, I hope."

"You *hope*, eh?"

They loped across the hills that were rapidly becoming white with snow. Jim found himself wondering about Mary. Maybe her father would worry about her if she did not return home for the night? He broached the question to her.

"He won't worry, Jim. I told him I might stay in town with Vivian Smith. Viv is about the only friend I have."

"I'm here now," Jim said. "Everything is under control."

"Oh, sure, yes!"

Jim had to smile. He found himself liking and admiring this girl more and more. She had been pretty frigid to him when he first saw her at the hotel, but there was something to be said for her attitude and her independence. She was good-natured and happy, but he judged that she wouldn't stand for being pushed around by anyone. The colour of her hair told him that much.

"You oughta play up to them Talbot boys. Somebody told me they were both single. You could wrap them around your little finger."

"Like I'm wrapping you, eh?"

"Jes' like you're wrappin' me," Jim said.

By the time they got to the herd, the Bucking Horse riders had it bedded down for the night. The cattle, although leg-tired, were spooky. This was a new range for them, and they were suspicious of anything that moved. A rider came out of the snow-filled world, hand raised.

"Jim," said a voice.

"This way, Bronc."

Bronc Thomas was a wiry, thin man of at least sixty. He had been ramrod for Jim's dad for years. He curbed his horse, snow on his beard, and he said, "How's ol' Len?"

"In a wheelchair."

Bronc Thomas peered at Jim with sharp blue eyes. "Trouble?" he asked.

"Ambush, a range war," Jim said. "But before I tell you about that, meet my little girl friend, Miss Mary Jones."

Despite the falling snow, Bronc Thomas took off his hat, showing a dome as bald as a billiard ball. "You work fast, Jim."

"She works even faster," Jim said. "Meet Len's *segundo* Broken Nose. How is the herd?"

"Itchy in the hoofs. They don't like it at all. Must be the wolves. All you see are wolves and coyotes, slinkin' in the distance. Now tell me about ol' Len?"

Jim told his foreman the news as they rode into camp. When the riders out on guard saw their boss they came pelting in to see what was new. Jim immediately held a council of war. The snow and wind were increasing both in velocity and in amount. Texas riders, wearing coats and overshoes, hunkered under the bed and grubwagon, listening. But most of the time their eyes, Jim noticed, were on Mary.

"How about winter range?" Bronc Thomas asked, when Jim had finished telling about the Talbots, the farmers, and about old Len. "Do we have grass for winter grazin'?"

"Damned little," Jim said. "Len has a little hay in stacks, but not much—just enough mebbe for his own stock. Mary's dad has a pretty big stack of wheat straw. He might sell part of that, she says."

"Can we graze them out on range?" a cowpuncher asked. "Head them into the high country and graze them north?"

"Be about our only bet," Jim said.

Two of his riders were crowding close to Mary, who sat beside the big hind wheel of the bed wagon. One of them, unseen by the girl, had winked at Jim, who had discreetly returned the wink.

Before Mary realised what was happening, a Texan was on each side of her, pressing close to her. She couldn't move. She was neatly sandwiched.

One of the men, a tall man named Slim, had a twinkle in his eye as he said, "Gotta keep you warm, little girl."

The other, a short man called Shorty, said, "Can't let you freeze to death, honey."

Mary looked from one to the other. Then she started to laugh. "I've got a lot of friends," she said. "All male, all Texan."

Jim said, "They're both married."

Shorty said, sadly, "Yes, but our wives —God bless them—are both dead."

"What happened?" Mary asked.

Slim was dripping melancholy. "We had to shoot them both. They went into a saloon and foundered on beer. Don't you ever read the newspapers?"

Mary looked at Slim's tragic face and then at Shorty's lonesome-looking features.

"Two of the ugliest men I've ever met," she told the crew.

Shorty drew himself up to his full

height of five feet four. "I'm mortified," he said. "My heart's busted and I'm all caved in. I'm goin' to sit over there."

As he moved away Slim followed up. "An unkind cut if ever I heerd one. It slashed me to the quick, Miss Mary. I'm agoin' ter leave yer."

"Good," said Mary with a roguish smile.

The crew laughed. Mary did not know it at that time, but by her humour and good spirits she had made herself very welcome in the Bucking Horse trailherd camp.

Jim got to his feet. "Well, you know the deal, all of you. They've already forced me to kill one man. It was his life or mine. We bed down here tonight and tomorrow we move, come snow, high-water or hell fire."

Slim looked at him. "How about the guard, boss?"

"Double guard. Ride in pairs, keep Winchesters handy."

Bronc Thomas said, "Okay, men, to your jobs. Remember what Jim said—

Winchesters handy. Short guns buckled on the outside of overcoats. Ike and Marty, ride with Slim and Shorty until midnight."

"All right, Bronc."

They rode into the falling snow. Texas men, faithful men, men born to saddle leather, the catch-rope, the smell of branding-irons. Cattle men, every inch of them. Moving into a strange range. Still, the high hope of adventure burned in their tired eyes.

With the coming of Mary, fatigue seemed to have left Jim's riders. And he hardly blamed them. He himself got a lift out of talking to her. Beside being attractive, she had a good mind and a level head. They crowded around her, joking and laughing, and she returned their banter. Bronc Thomas and Jim hunkered alone, talking about the trip ahead. Broken Nose, being a wise man, was talking with the cook, who was working with his dutch ovens over his fire, the snow dying as it hit his hot fire.

Finally chuck time came and they ate,

and later Mary helped the cook wash up. The men made a bunk for her in the bed wagon which was covered by a sunaged tarp. The wind died down, the snow stopped falling, and the first thing Jim knew somebody was shaking him as he lay in his blankets.

"Four in the morning, Jim."

"Okay, Bronc."

Bronc had snow on his overcoat. He said, "Texas men and Texas cattle—longhorns both. Outcasts they are on Montana grass. Me for a bit of shut-eye. Is that girl stirring in her wagon, Jim?"

From behind the canvas came Mary's voice. "I ride one guard shift, anyway. After all, I came out here to see a trailherd move."

Soon she and Jim were riding out to the herd. Cattle were restless and hungry, and they were starting to move of their own accord. Dry cows made up the most part of the herd. They had calved on the trail and the crew had butchered the calves or had given them to farmers. Calves held back a trail herd. Jim figured he would get bulls from Len, and there was, therefore, no point in moving bulls north, too.

Already longhorn cows were moving North, grazing as they moved. The high bunch and Buffalo grass was dry and unappetising and in other circumstances the cattle would not have looked at it. It was this or nothing and the cattle knew it.

Jim said, "Jus' mosey along, Mary. Let them move of their own accord. They've got lots of miles behin' them. . . ."

"Gee, look at them."

Five thousand odd head of cattle, surly and ugly and tired, yet stringy and tough and sturdy. Many had died on the trail; truly, a survival of the fittest. They moved like wind moving across high grass, backs bobbing.

Mary said, "Here comes a rider, Jim. From the direction of town."

Jim spurred forward to meet him. Mary rode with him, and then she said to Jim, "That's ol' man Wilson, the swamper. He and Dad are good friends. Now what is he doing out here—?"

Jim saw that the old man's face was blue with cold. His hands, gripping the bridle-reins, shook but it was hard to say whether the cold or excitement was the cause.

"Mary! Thank God, I found you, child!"

"Mr. Wilson! What in heaven's name brings you out here—on a day like this?"

The old man panted. "I hate to have to tell you this. But your farm house burned down last night!"

Jim glanced at Mary and saw how pale she had gone.

"Yes—what else?"

"Your father—he died in it!"

9

Riders in the Night

THEY rode a mile out of Branding Iron. Then without warning Bowie Talbot reined in his horse.

"I'm ridin' back to town, Knife. I'm goin' to hang onto Linklatter's tail; he might try to run. We got to have them deeds first. They're due in on tomorrow's stage. We need Linklatter until we get them deeds."

Knife nodded, seeing the logic of his brother's plan. "An' I cain't see no use after all of plantin' some of Jim Rathburn's belongin's on him. We'll hit Jim's herd afore it comes into Milk River valley an' scatter it to hell an' gone!"

Bowie listened, head canted.

Knife continued with, "Linklatter will ride with us and they'll find him dead, shot durin' the stampede. That will put his death on Rathburn's shoulders."

Bowie nodded, eyes shining. "Good idea, Knife. Well, I'll head back to town. Meet you at Sunken Springs about midnight. An' Linklatter'll be with me."

"You'd both better be there, for damn' sure!"

"Don't fret yourself. We'll be there right enough and with our guns on."

Bowie Talbot reined his bronc around. "Bring me out a fresh cayuse. Have him at the line camp. This hoss is gettin' tired."

"I'll see to it."

Bowie said, "I'm still wonderin' about Mary. I'd hate to have her hurt."

"Hang onto yourself! Is she more valuable than Milk River basin? You can always get another filly—even a squaw—"

Bowie loped away, returning to Branding Iron. Knife Talbot rode on to the Heart Nine outfit. This was the slack period of the year, for beef round-up was over. Most of his crew had been paid off and had left, going south to work in a warmer climate for the winter. He had a crew of five men who would feed hay to cattle during the long winter months. They were picked men, not only experts at working with cattle but retained because each knew how to handle a Winchester and short-gun. Knife stomped into the kitchen and put on the coffee pot.

A man looked in, said, "Howdy, Knife."

"How goes the spread, Ole."

"Good. When is the bobwire comin' out?"

Knife poured coffee into the pot. "Be out in the morning. The hardware man is haulin' it out. Then we get to work stringin' wire."

"We need help."

"We're gettin' it. Hired four new men in town this afternoon. They can handle a rifle as good as they can string wire."

"How about thet farmer named Jones?"

Knife looked at the rider. "Well, what about him?" he enquired.

"Has he told yet?"

"You ask too many questions, Ole. You just work here and don't forget that. Now get outa here an' stay out."

Ole's grin hid his anger. "You sound like you got a new saddle sore," he said, and left.

As he made coffee Knife thought about Mary. Too bad that a woman had to be involved in what was to happen. He knew very little about women. His mother had died too long ago to be remembered.

He and Bowie had been on their own when mere children. They had worked together, fought together, fought each other. They had gone outside of the law together. But that had been in Old Mexico. They had made a quick stake by robbing mine-trains of bullion. Then, in Dodge City, they had bought a trail herd, had pushed north into Montana. And so had incurred the anger of old Len Rathburn.

Knife remembered the days when he and Bowie had robbed and killed. But Old Mexico was far away, plenty far, and nobody in Montana knew what they had done. The main thing now was to get control of Milk River valley. So far they had outguessed Len Rathburn. They had deeds to a strip of land across the middle of Bucking Horse range.

Only Jones stood between them and a drift fence that would imprison Bucking Horse cattle on the poorest grass on the range. And when the blizzards came Len's cattle would be helpless and starve to death. When spring came their bodies would be piled high against the barbed wire and that would be the end of Len, too.

In the living room, turned yellow by the light of a kerosene lamp, Knife picked up a magazine and read for a while. About eleven o'clock he looked at the clock and then threw the magazine down and went out to the tool-shed. There, he picked up a five-gallon can of kerosene and took it with him to the barn, where he dropped it into a sack, before tying it to the saddle of a second horse he intended taking along with him.

Shortly afterwards he headed for Sunken Springs.

The snow swirled in and the night was intensely cold. The distance to Sunken Springs was about ten miles and it was round about midnight when Knife reached the spot. There was no light showing from a cabin that was set back in the high cottonwoods that were now losing their leaves.

He rode in and silently dismounted, leaving his bronc in the high buck-brush. He didn't enter the cabin, but squatted outside the windbreak, back to the wall, waiting patiently.

After a while two riders came out of the night.

"This way," said Knife as he got to his feet.

Bowie said, "Where is my fresh cayuse?"

"In the brush with my horse. Take them both out, eh?" Knife turned to look at Martin Linklatter, who had remained in the saddle. "How goes it?" he asked. "Winter is here."

"For a while, I reckon. Snow won't last but a few days. Too early for winter to set in yet."

Bowie returned with the two broncs. He unsaddled his own and threw the equipment over the fresh horse. "The girl is not at the farm tonight," he told his brother. "She rode out with the Texan."

"With whom?"

Bowie tied his latigo and swung himself up. "You heard me! With the young Texan, Rathburn. She wants to see how a trail herd is moved . . . or somethin' like that. Looks like somebody's cuttin' you out, Knife!"

Hoisting himself into the saddle Knife remarked, "It sure breaks my heart, it does. Anyhow I'm glad she's not there. I don't cotton to the idea of moving against a woman."

"Since when did you go soft?" asked his brother.

"Damn it, a woman's a woman whether she happens to be Mary or not! Don't forgit that if we killed Mary, or any other woman for that matter, the range would be against us."

Linklatter said, "You're right there, Knife."

Bowie gave them the curt order to ride and they headed through the brush, heads down against the wind. Bowie was in the lead and followed by his brother and then Linklatter. The men could hear the splash of the kerosene in the can but nobody spoke.

They rode across country and the night's darkness hid the evil in them. Bowie pushed his fresh horse and appeared unconcerned at what lay before him, but Linklatter was thinking of a warm bed and the money he had stowed in his office. The mind of Knife Talbot dwelt on Len Rathburn, and how they had ambushed him, and soon his thoughts turned to Jim Rathburn. Len's nephew had challenged him to pull his gun and he knew that he had been afraid and had welcomed the intervention of Sheriff Harden.

Within a half hour, they were in the

bluffs back of the Jones' farm. They drew rein and leaned on the forks of their saddles and looked down at a house they could not see because of the darkness.

Bowie said, "The girl has a dog."

Knife replied, "She keeps him in the house, she told me. He's just a pup. The coyotes are hungry for the pup and she knows it."

"The joint is dark," Linklatter said.

Bowie Talbot answered sourly, "Hell, we got eyes . . . too, Linklatter." He went down and Linklatter heard a Winchester rifle slide out of its leather saddle-holster. "Get the can, Knife."

Knife Talbot dismounted and untied the can, mumbling as the cold wind hit his bare hands.

Martin Linklatter said, "You don't need me. I'll stay and hold the broncs. Two of you is enough for that little job."

Bowie Talbot whipped his bulk around, looked hard at the land locator. Finally he said, "Logic in that. Horses might stray. Might stampede if there is any gunfire.

But make damn sure you'll be here when we come back, Linklatter."

"You don't trust me?"

"Not one cockeyed inch, Linklatter."

Knife growled, "Can the fool talk, an' let's git goin'."

They went into the snowstorm, bent against the wind. When they got closer to the house they could make out its outlines. They stopped by the hen house.

"Sprinkle the kerosene around the base, and light it," Bowie said. "I'll stay here with a rifle."

The dog, inside the house, started to bark. Knife moved forward, unscrewing the cork of the can as he did so. Suddenly the back door opened and the dog ran out, followed by Mary's father, who was armed. He went in the direction taken by Knife, but only for a short distance, for it was then that Bowie got a bead on him and fired almost at once. The Winchester made a hard, a clean sound in the wind. The bullet found its mark and when he hit the ground Lester Jones was dead.

The pup had caught up with Knife and

wanted to play with him. Knife was flattened against the wall and he kicked out as the dog who rolled over, yelped and then scurried away. Knife went round the corner of the house and almost fell over the body of the murdered man.

Knife called out, "You killed him, gunman."

Bowie Talbot came forward, rifle under his arm. Lester Jones wore only long-handled underwear. Evidently he had been in bed when the dog had awakened him. Bowie picked up the man's rifle.

"Take him inside and throw him on the bed. We leave his rifle in there, too. We'll burn the carcass."

They went inside. Knife Talbot threw the limp body of Lester Jones on the bed. Bowie put the rifle beside the man he had murdered. Knife went out and returned with the can. He began sprinkling the kerosene around until the room was saturated. He threw a light inside from the porch.

By the time they reached the ridge

Martin Linklatter was in the saddle. "What was the shootin' about?"

Knife Talbot said, "Jones is dead."

"Who—shot him?"

Knife's horse reared against the bit. "Nobody shot him, you damn fool! Jones shot hisself. He committed suicide. Laid on the bed, put the rifle to his head—got his toe in the trigger . . . Bullet went right through his head!"

Linklatter grinned. "Second shot sounded kinda muffled, like it had been fired inside the house."

Bowie snarled, "We had to leave a empty ca'tridge in his Winchester to make it look like suicide. Let's head outa here pronto! Somebody'll see the fire an' ride hell fer leather to investigate."

They came to the fork in the trail and Linklatter said, "I ride for town. So long, men."

Bowie Talbot replied, "We ride in with you. We got to stay close to the pulse of this thing, and that pulse is Brandin' Iron town."

They rode toward town. Three riders,

pushing through the night, heading across Milk River valley.

Suddenly Knife said, “Wonder where thet pup vamoosed to?”

Bowie looked back. “Cain’t see him follerin’ up. We cain’t afford to have him trail us.”

They continued on through drifting snow and behind them the Jones house was wrapped in flames.

Again Knife said, “Where the hell did thet pup get to?”

“I dunno,” Bowie replied crossly. “But I know one thing—he ain’t follerin’ us. Ride an’ keep your mouth shut.”

10

Dead Man's Range

BY the time Jim and Mary reached the Jones' farm, the thermometer had sunk to below zero. Snow came with blasts of wind, and Jim felt a touch of fear—if this kept up the winter would be terribly long, coming this early in the year. And the longer the winter the more cattle he would lose.

The trip down the rimrock trail had been a rough one. Already ice and snow covered the narrow defile down which only one bronc could go at a time. Once Mary's horse had slipped, almost throwing itself and girl over the cliff, but the bronc had caught his footing in time. So badly did the girl want to reach the farm that she took the lead on the trail, riding as quickly as the treacherous footing would permit. There was danger in every step.

Finally, they reached the bottom. And Jim, turning in saddle, looked back at the trail, already being snowed shut.

"Is that the only trail down into Milk River valley, Mary?"

"The only one—so they tell me."

Jim nodded, eyes sombre. "Cattle can't go down there now. Snow is too deep, and the footing too slippery. It looks to me my cattle won't reach Milk River valley—unless we have a thaw."

"You'll be lucky if you can get back on the ridge to your cattle," Wilson said. "If this snow keeps on, thet narrow pass will be snowed plumb shut. The drifts can run to as high as thirty feet."

They were on the plain and Mary pushed on ahead, her quirt rising and falling. They came into Branding Iron, now coated with glistening snow, and a man hollered, "Sheriff Harden is out at your place, Mary."

"Thank you," she called back.

Martin Linklatter stood in his office

and watched through the window, warm and secure beside the stove. His eyes met those of Jim.

The men stared at each other in open hostility, each recognising the other for an enemy. Linklatter's face suddenly looked glum.

They rode past the Broken Stirrup Saloon. Knife Talbot could be seen through the front window. He stood beside the stove. Jim could clearly see the interior of the saloon.

Bowie Talbot was not inside.

"First time I've ever seen them skunks separated," he told Mary.

Wilson said, "The end of my ride. . . . A whisky bottle for this boy." He turned his bronc toward the Broken Stirrup.

Mary and Jim rode on. The thought came to Jim that this was a tough time for the Talbots to start their drift fence. The ground was freezing and soon digging a posthole would be almost impossible. It would be deadly cold for men to work with shovels and barbed wire and staples and posts.

Jim said nothing to Mary. He remembered when his father and his brother had been shot down. But he, being a man, had been more resistant to the shock; she, a slip of a woman, was breaking slowly.

He looked around him. The range was filled with snow that clung to sagebrush, covering them.

"Damn this damn snow!"

"A person can't fight nature, Jim."

Jim showed a wry smile. "Only thing a man can do is wait . . . and hope. My heart goes out to you, Mary."

"I know it does, Jim."

They came to the farmstead. There were some rigs and saddled horses standing around, and people looking at the ruins.

Mary dismounted, walked over to Sheriff Harden, who stood poking in some ashes. "Where is his body, sheriff?"

The sheriff looked at her, eyes full of pity. "I'm sorry, girl," he said, his sunken eyes mirroring genuine sorrow.

"He lies in that wagon yonder—with a tarp over him."

She started toward the wagon. He grabbed her by the forearm. She stopped and said, "I want to see him."

"He isn't good to look at, Mary."

"He's my father, my only kin."

Sheriff Harden kept his grip on her. "Don't look at him, the bullet hit him in the head—"

"Who killed him?"

Harden let his hand drop. "I don't know if anybody killed him. His rifle was close to his body. One cartridge in it—the one in the barrel—was empty. Had he ever mentioned—suicide?"

"Suicide!"

Mary's voice was sharp, almost a cry. Her hand went to her mouth, her eyes became agonized pools of terror. Jim watched in silence, feeling her sorrow and surprise. Sheriff Harden's sunken eyes were on her.

"You mean—he might have—killed himself, Sheriff?"

"That could be so, Miss Mary. Of

course, a coroner's inquest will affix the cause of death, and I have to wait for that."

"He never killed himself!"

"Did he ever suggest that he might end it all?"

"Never, never."

Bowie Talbot was standing close by. He looked at Jim for a moment and their eyes met. For all that Talbot showed in the glance he was looking at a complete stranger Jim smiled at him provokingly.

Talbot was not playing however. He just stood there and listened and watched. Jim was, of course, well aware that nobody had a better reason for killing Jones and burning his property than the Talbot brothers. The question was whether anything could be proved against them.

Jim had a look round the place in the hope of coming across a clue of some sort, but the wind and the snow had covered every possible track, if indeed murder and arson had been done. Plenty of people had tramped about the place once the fire had been discovered.

Glancing at the bluffs behind the farm site Jim got up on his horse and rode up the slope. He had no better luck there. The snow had come down to blot everything out, and had heightened the mystery surrounding the grisly end of Mary's father.

Cold from the raw wind, he rode back to the farmstead. The wagon carrying the body of Lester Jones was moving towards Branding Iron. Mary was still talking to the Sheriff. Bowie Talbot stood to one side, glowering and mean-looking. Jim would have ignored him had not Talbot spoken.

"You lose somethin' back in the hills, Rathburn?"

Jim turned and looked at him. "You look like you been without sleep for a night or so, Talbot." He made his words carry a hidden meaning.

Sheriff Harden turned and said, "No trouble between you two! I've been watchin' both of you and if either of you makes a move toward the other." He moved over and got between them.

Jim said, "I looked for horse and man sign on the hill. This could have been a deliberate fire and a deliberate killin'."

Harden said hurriedly, "No imputations, Rathburn, if you please. I try to ride a middle-course and you boys are tryin' to push me off. I favour neither of you. Your uncle Len had no love for this farmer either, Rathburn.

"He's in a wheelchair," Jim reminded the Sheriff.

Harden wouldn't be gainsaid however. "This has gone far enough," he said shortly. With a grim, determined mien he warned both men. "I'll use a gun if necessary," he said without hesitation.

Jim feared neither the Sheriff nor Bowie Talbot, and he looked at Mary who slowly shook her head. He realized, then, that the girl had, in the last few hours, suffered enough from excitement and shock; he decided not to add to her distress and he moved away, going toward the barn.

A team of mules and milk cow were in the barn. He milked the cow and then untied the mules and drove them with the cow out of the barn. By the time he had done these chores, most of the onlookers had left.

Jim went to where Harden stood with Mary.

Jim said, "So Bowie Talbot left, eh?" Harden nodded.

Jim Rathburn went on, "So help me Sheriff, if he or his brother get in my way, I'm killin' them—or they're killin' me. I can't forget thet beatin' in the hotel room—two against one—"

"You have no evidence they did it, Rathburn."

Jim said, "They did it. They had the gall to ride into the Buckin' Horse an' call me again. They sent the bullet through the belly of my uncle and put him in that wheelchair. They'd've killed Len, had they been lucky."

"Don't git too rough, Rathburn!"

Jim paid no attention to the lawman's warning. "They put thet gunman on me.

Sure, I can't prove it—but the man was a stranger."

"You can't prove he worked for the Talbots."

"Sure I can't. But I can tell you this—if either of them two move against me, I'm pullin' my gun against them with intent. I'm layin' this on the line now and here!"

Sheriff Harden scowled. "You make yourself clear, Rathburn," he said. He spoke to Mary. "My sympathy is with you, girl. What do you aim to do?"

"I—I don't know, yet."

"I'm sure there's folks around you'll be able to stay with."

"Thank you. I might do that—I'm sort of upset now."

The sheriff moved away, going towards the barn. Mary looked at Jim. "Thanks for ridin' here with me, Jim. But they might need you back at your herd . . . if you can get back there over the rimrock trail."

Jim looked at the scarp ridge to the south. Now covered with snow, it made a formidable barrier: it locked the valley in its grip, holding it in snowy steepness. He could not see the trail for snow which had even covered the great rocks which stood sentinel over it.

"I'll have to buck snow to get back there. Are you riding to town or are you staying here a while and going with Sheriff Harden?"

"I'll ride in with him. Wonder where my dog is?"

Jim looked at her. "Your—dog?"

"Yes, my puppy. The collie. Wonder if he perished in the fire? We always kept him indoors at night."

"Do you want me to go into the house and have a look round?"

"Yes, I would like to know what happened to the dog."

Moving around the burnt out wreckage, which had cooled off, Jim came across two iron bedsteads, twisted by the heat into grotesque shapes. After poking around for some time Jim returned to Mary.

"If the dog had died in there," he

explained, I think I should have come across some trace of him."

"He must have got away."

Jim considered this. A pup might follow the men or riders who had set fire to a house. A pup might follow anybody, for that matter, when afraid and lonesome. Jim was sure that the fire had not been accidental. When the Talbots wanted something, they went after it. He was sure that similar doubts and fears were with Mary Jones. . . .

"He should be around," Jim said.

She whistled and called, but the pup did not come out of the brush. Sheriff Harden, returning from a tour of the premises, said he had not seen the dog. Jim silently cursed the snow, which had started to fall again.

"Wonder if he went to the Heart Nine outfit," Jim said to Harden.

Harden turned sharply, thin against the grey day, and gave him a long look. "Why should the pup go over to the Talbot spread, Rathburn?"

"Might have followed them."

"Are you implying that they are responsible for this?"

"That's just what I am suggesting."

"How about Lester Jones? In bed, bullet hole through his head, rifle beside him with a fired cartridge?"

"That doesn't make it suicide," Jim said.

Harden said, "Don't assert somethin' you can't prove."

Jim smiled a little. "They rode over here yesterday, Mary says. They wanted to buy Lester Jones out so they could run their drift fence through his property. He wouldn't sell."

Harden nodded, said, "She told me about that. You still haven't proved anything. For a warrant you need proof not suspicion."

Jim said, "That's the outline, sheriff. If the dog has followed them to the Heart Nine, would you look upon that as evidence?"

"Not necessarily."

"And why not?"

"A dog can stray in any direction. You

say they want this farm because they want to run bobwire acrost it. All right, that's so—but do they automatically get it, seein' this house burned down, seein' Lester Jones is dead?" He answered his own question. "The place will go to Mary. It won't go to the Talbots."

"But I'll have to sell," Mary pointed out. "I can't farm this place, I haven't money to build a new house. We had only thirty some dollars, Dad and I, and it went up in that fire—I'm destitute."

Harden spoke to her. "Then if the Talbots offer to buy this spread you'll have to sell to them?"

"Yes, I have to get rid of it now."

In the midst of this talk Jim looked up and saw a wagon approaching. Squaw sat on the seat, driving a team of greys. A couple of old blankets covered her wide bulk and turned the wind and snow. She had got Len's wheelchair on to the wagon and secured it with ropes.

Len Rathburn had on a big long sheepskin coat. Jim stared at his uncle. But it was not Len's appearance that surprised him. What surprised him was that sitting beside the old rider's wheelchair was a collie dog. A pup.

"There's my pup!" Mary said.

Len Rathburn said, "Your pup drifted over to our place this mornin', Miss Jones. Seemed scared as all git out. Then one of my riders came in and told me about your misfortune, so we decided to bring the pup to you."

The dog leaped down, ran to Mary. She knelt and hugged him. Jim looked at the Sheriff and smiled tightly.

"There goes one of my theories," he said.

"Sure busts it to smithereens."

Len Rathburn looked at them in a puzzled manner. "What are you two hellions talkin' about?" he asked.

"Nothin'." Jim grinned. "Nothin'! Len."

11

Rifles in the Snow

BOOTS pounded across the slivery plank floor. The fire in the pot-bellied soft-coal heater spread its warmth. Martin Linklatter sat behind his desk and looked at Knife Talbot who walked the floor, big-knuckled hands locked behind his broad back.

From where he sat, the land locator could see the main street of Branding Iron town.

"Here comes the cadaver now," Linklatter said.

Knife Talbot stopped walking, turned sharply to look out the frost-rimmed window. A wagon creaked into town, iron-rimmed wheels crunching the snow. It went slowly down the street to stop in front of a small log building used as a morgue.

Knife Talbot said, "Well, Lester Jones knows the answer, now. Though he had to learn the hard way . . . Wonder where thet pup went?"

"Oh, forget the damned pup!"

Knife looked at the man with slow determination rising in his pale eyes. "If that pup goes to the Heart Nine, it will look bad for us—people will figure he follered us."

"Forget it Knife, there's nothing to worry about."

Knife again turned his attention to the wagon. Three men were carrying the body of Lester Jones into the cold interior of the log building. They had the body on planks.

"Two stiffs in there now," Martin Linklatter said.

Knife nodded. "Layin' him alongside the drifter that we hired to kill this young Rathburn button. He sat around the bunkhouse out at the Heart Nine and bragged about how he could outshoot anybody what walked. Wonder if anybody knows that he hung around our spread a few days before he tackled his last chore?"

"Doubt it, Knife."

Knife said, "There they come out. Goin' into a saloon for a drink. Where in the hell is Bowie?"

"Maybe he is still talking to Mary Jones."

Knife nodded, eyes thoughtful. "Hope he can buy that Jones farm. She should sell. She's alone an' she's flat busted."

"Bowie should be able to fix it."

Knife watched the snow falling on Branding Iron's main street. But as he watched he was thinking of other things. Particularly his ambition, and Bowie's of course, to secure control of Milk River valley. The drift fence was the key to the whole situation, for it would contain the Bucking Horse cattle in an area too small for survival. The brothers were not only greedy but cunning.

They both realised for instance that the West, to a certain degree, was becoming more settled. Nowadays things had to be done according to the book, at least anything that was done had to appear legal and valid. Hence the plan to run the drift fence from one side of the valley to the other, the posts anchored to land to which they owned the deeds.

Everything looked certain to shape up until the arrival of Jim Rathburn but with his coming, followed by 5,000 head of cattle, the entire picture had changed. The spotlight had shifted and Knife understood only too well that a dangerous new factor had now challenged their calculations.

"His herd is snowed in, Martin," Knife Talbot said. "He can't come off the rimrock until warm weather opens the trail."

"Nor can he go up to his cattle," the land locator said. "Unless he swings way around about twenty miles, and goes up the Larb Crick side of the rimrock."

Knife growled, "A man can't stampede cattle that are snowed-in. They'll die up there with no hay. Jes' hope thet the snow an' col' weather keeps up."

"Be good for us."

Knife said, "Wish Bowie would come in."

Linklatter swung his polished boots onto his desk. He was bored with this big blundering cowpuncher. He tried to hide his dislike by looking at his boots.

He had to get out of Milk River Valley, for he realised only too well that he was now a thorn in the side of the Talbots. They would put the chill on him whenever it suited their purpose. He knew too much about them, and they, and the neighbouring farmers, had paid him well for his services.

Linklatter glanced at the safe which contained a tidy little fortune. It gave him comfort, but he couldn't help thinking of the fate that had overtaken Lester Jones. How he had run out of his cabin and the coldness with which Bowie had killed the farmer. Murder didn't worry Bowie, nor his brother.

Knife interrupted his meditations. "How about the stage?" he enquired.

Linklatter lifted his eyes slowly. "Might get through. Depends on how deep the snow is in Tank Coulee. Even so the deeds may not have been sent yet."

"They'd better be."

"Nothing we can do if they ain't, at least not yet." Linklatter sensed the threat in Knife's question and he knew he was safe from the brothers as long as the deeds did not reach the office. The Talbots might be fast on the trigger but they understood little about the law.

When the deeds came they would be through with him—he would have served their purpose and he would then be in real peril. Linklatter shifted uneasily until he realised that not until Mary sold out to the brothers would they finally have no need of him. That was something to remember, even if the stage got through with the deeds that would allow the brothers to get a start on the fence. If only Mary refused to sell out he would be safe.

The irony of the situation struck him. Here he was plotting against the very men with whom he should be co-operating.

"Wonder where Sheriff Harden is?" Knife Talbot asked.

Linklatter replied, "A lost dog sniffin' up the wrong stump, that's Harden. Why don't he die an' git it over with?"

"Been sick for years . . . they tell me."

"Bad heart, they say. If he gets in our way there must be some way to make his heart click out on him."

The stove crackled. The wind rose suddenly, screeched in the eaves, then, just as suddenly, it died down. The Montana rangelands lay white and deadly cold under the snow. Elk and deer were drifting down from the high peaks, going to lower levels where snow was not as deep and where grass could more easily be pawed loose. The bears slept in their lairs, deep in hibernation. Winter had suddenly descended.

"Here comes Harden an' Bowie now," Knife Talbot said, excitement rimming his words.

Linklatter looked out of the window without leaving his swivel chair. "Look at Harden," he said, "large as life an' twice as ugly. Anyhow, Bowie seems on good terms with him, which is just as well."

"Bowie's a smart one," said his brother gloatingly.

They watched the pair ride by. Harden dismounted in front of the court-house. Bowie Talbot rode into the livery-barn. Soon a boy came out of the court-house, took Harden's horse into the barn.

Without warning, the back door suddenly opened. Bowie Talbot entered, beating snow from him. He wore overshoes over his boots and had mittens on. A bandanna was tied around his ears, knotted under his jaw. He beat the snow from his hat against his sheekskin chaps.

"You'll get the floor sloppy an' dirty," Linklatter growled.

Talbot's eyes became flecked with anger. "Go to hell!"

Linklatter smiled, with his lips only. "Take it easy, friend." Deliberately he hid his anger under a cloak of discretion. "Somethin' go wrong out to the Jones homestead, Bowie?"

"Plenty."

Alarm showed in Knife Talbot's face. His lips trembled. "They—they get wise we—kilt him, Bowie?" Logic came to his rescue and he said, "But you an' the Sheriff rode into town together. Quit scarin' the hell outa me, Bowie!"

Bowie Talbot hung his hat on the rack. "They're not wise. Harden still claims it was suicide."

Knife asked, "The dog—He made his way to the Heart Nine outfit? He gave us away, maybe—?"

"He's got that pup on the brain," exclaimed Linklatter.

Bowie smiled, the gesture not fitting his mood. "The dog did not go to the Heart Nine, my good-lookin' brother. He went to the Buckin' Horse outfit an' ol' Len an' Squaw returned him to Mary Jones."

"What did the Sheriff say?"

"Say? About what?" Bowie asked.

"About the dog goin' to the Rathburn spread. Did he bring up the idea that mebbe Len Rathburn ordered somebody to gun Jones an' the dog followed the killers back home?"

"I mentioned that to Harden as we rode into town."

"What did he say?" Knife asked.

"Nothing. I left the idea with him, that's all."

Linklatter asked, "Did you talk with Mary about selling?"

Bowie moved over to the stove. He put his back to it and warmed his hands behind his body.

"That's what gets me so mad. Jim Rathburn he hung onto her like a tick hangs onto a sick cow. I never got a chance to talk to her. A man can't just bust up to a woman feelin' as bad as she did an' suddenly ask her to sell. Not when mebbe the finger of suspicion points to him as a possible murderer of her ol' man."

"Right," Linklatter said.

Bowie looked at his brother. "The stage is comin' through. We saw it from the summit of Croden's Ridge. Makin' slow time, but comin' ahead."

"Hope the deeds are there," Linklatter said.

"Where is Mary now," Knife asked.

"She went with the Rathburns to the Buckin' Hoss' spread. That Jim sure ties onto her like he means business."

"What if they talk her into selling her land to them?" asked Knife. "That sure would put the caboose on our plan."

"I've thought of that," replied Bowie. "But what could I do? You can't just walk over to a girl, grab her an' keep her from goin' somewhere she has a mind to go to, can you?"

"It doesn't look too good," answered his brother.

Bowie nodded but said, "I doubt if she'll sell to them. She's stubborn, that girl. But if she does want a buyer we must have a chance, 'cause she'll want as much dinero as she can get for it. She's smart and might do business with us after all."

Knife rubbed his scar. "Hope you're right," he said. Through the window he noticed the arrival of the stage and, having drawn the attention of the others to it, said, "I'll go over to the post office an' see what mail we have."

Linklatter stood up. "I'll go with you," he volunteered.

"No need for you to go out," Knife said. "You an' Bowie talk this thing over some more. I'll bring in the mail."

"Maybe the postmaster won't hand it over to you."

Knife studied the land locator and gave him an odd look. "Are you all there today?" he asked. "The postmaster handed over the mail before and he'll do it again."

Linklatter shrugged his shoulders and Knife opened the door letting in a gust of cold air and swirling snowflakes.

Bowie moved over to the stove and stood with his back to it. He seemed to be talking to himself. "We got them at a standstill," he said slowly. "Jim Rathburn can't move the cattle down the rimrock trail because the snow is too deep. Ol' Mother Nature came an' gave us a helpin' hand."

Linklatter was silent, his thoughts on the deeds. It was bad luck that the Talbots had happened to be around just when the stagecoach came in, otherwise he might have been able to destroy them and nobody would have been the wiser. It would have made him feel safer.

Bowie was still talking to himself. "You can't stampede cattle with the snow up to their bellies. It ain't necessary to do a darn thing about it."

"They'll starve to death," put in Linklatter.

Bowie nodded. "If this weather holds Jim Rathburn will be out of business."

Knife was quickly back with some letters and a small package. "Here they are," he said triumphantly, throwing the package at Linklatter. "From the office of the territorial land agent in Helena, and I'll eat my shirt if them deeds ain't in it."

Linklatter's hands trembled as he broke the string binding the parcel, but the brothers imagined it was with excitement.

"It's the deeds without a doubt. Wonder if they are all here? I'll check them against the names of the homesteaders."

He did so carefully and found what he

feared. The deeds were complete and now all the land, with the exception of the Jones strip, belonged to the Talbot Heart Nine outfit.

"We gotta get the girl to sell," Knife said jubilantly.

Bowie replied, "We can start our drift fence an' work towards her place. Be about six miles of fence to put in before we reach her property and by that time she should have sold it to us."

Linklatter's brows rose. "Working—in this storm—?"

"Snow or no snow, cold or no cold—we put in drift fence," Bowie Talbot answered. "Okay, Knife, let's git movin'!"

12

Snowbound Guns

A BIG cottonwood log burned in the fireplace made of native Montana stone. Mary Jones sat cross-legged on the floor, her pup beside her.

"I can't believe it," she said. "He was alive yesterday, and well and strong, looking toward the future—"

Squaw said, "Drink this, girl."

Mary took the coffee. "It tastes bitter," she said as she drank it. She didn't know that the bitterness was caused by a stiff jolt of whisky. Squaw waddled back into her domain, her kitchen.

Len Rathburn sat in his wheelchair, looking at Mary, who stroked the smooth hair of the collie.

"There ain't nothin' this ol' rider can say, girl," the owner of the Bucking Horse Iron said gently. "You can never tell what goes on inside another man. Not even those smart college professors can do that, Miss Mary."

Mary lifted her eyes and looked at the old cowman. By now she had recovered her equilibrium somewhat, although the sense of shock and loss was still deep. She kept her voice steady.

"My father never shot himself, Mr. Rathburn. I knew him too well to believe he would ever do a thing like that. He was very religious and read the Bible every day of his life. Nobody will ever convince me that he laid hands upon himself."

Jim Rathburn, standing at the window, watched the snow outside, but his mind was not on the elements. He was listening to what Mary was saying. He recognised her quiet courage, and he knew whoever got her would get a good wife. He knew, too, that she wouldn't care how poor a man was if she loved him. She had it in her to make somebody happy, for apart from her undoubted good looks, he could tell she would never be other than loyal and constant.

Jim realised that he had yet to establish himself and his cattle, either on Milk River grass or across the border into Canada. Not until this problem was solved could he dare think about Mary although it would make no difference to her if she cared for him.

The red-headed cowpuncher was full of unease. Everything, it seemed, had gone against him. From the moment the Talbots had first attacked him he had been under pressure from men and events, and now the weather had become his enemy. His uncle had said that this was the earliest snowfall ever seen on Milk River, but what did it matter if the storm was out of the ordinary? It didn't help any.

You couldn't explain the vagaries of the seasons to his cattle, which were snowed in on the south benchlands. The only trail leading down to Milk River was blocked and by now, the drifts on the rimrock trail would be impassable. Cattle could not wallow through loose snow, and he wondered how many of them he would lose. It was a grim thought.

Jim consoled himself with the thought that his herd was tough, but the cattle were not accustomed to deep snow or such low temperature. It was a question of how much his longhorns could stand.

The girl and Len must have sensed how impatient and thwarted he felt because when he walked over to another window and looked out once more, their eyes were upon him.

"Jim," said Mary softly, with her cheeks flushed and her eyes bright and intelligent, "there is nothing that you can do about it."

The cowpuncher turned impatiently. "Here I am cooped up here while my cows are dying on the benchlands. They need hay to fight the cold."

"You can't get fodder up to them at this moment," Mary answered. "Unless the storm breaks and there is a thaw, they're going to be up there for some time, and you might just as well reconcile yourself to the situation."

"Oh, Lord," Jim groaned.

He could see them in his mind's eye: bunched, heads down, the blizzard would be howling and the snow moving in a thick cloud. And his Texan riders—faithful and, as yet, unpaid—would be crouched over small fires trying to keep from freezing to death. Jim understood their predicament only too well. They had grub certainly, but not too much, and he knew they could use more blankets. The men were more than just hired hands to him. They were his friends and companions and he felt he ought to be with them, sharing their privations.

Jim turned and faced Mary. "If only I could get some hay out to them," he said.

His uncle, who had so far not spoken said, "No one can be blamed for the moods of the weather."

Mary spoke again. "I'm sorry you came down with me," she said. "I guess you should have stayed at camp when the news came through about my father. You would have been happier there, doing what you could for your herd."

"I never meant it that way," replied Jim. "I couldn't let you ride without going with you. Anyhow Bronc knows his business and Broken Nose is up there with him."

As Squaw came in with a fresh pot of coffee a new thought came to Jim. He mulled it over in his mind, saw that Mary was watching him, and then looked at her and said, "You want to know what I'm thinking. All right, let's get down to brass tacks, but I'll have to ask you to bear with me a little, Mary, but maybe we could settle something here right now."

"You mean—about my homestead?" the girl asked.

Jim nodded. "The Talbots need it. They want it to finish their drift fence. Maybe they killed your father. We'll let that point ride unanswered for the present."

Squaw stood in the doorway, big and heavy, holding the coffee pot. Len Rathburn watched Jim, eyes puckered and sharp. Mary put down her cup because her hands had suddenly started to tremble.

"Go on, Jim," she said.

"Bowie Talbot was at your place, Mary, for one purpose—maybe two. If he and his gang set fire to your spread, then he came back to check. Secondly, I think he wanted to talk to you . . . alone."

"I believe that too, Jim. But when you pressed him, and made trouble for him, he changed his mind about seein' me alone. I think he intended to try to buy my land."

"Just guesswork," Len Rathburn said.

Jim replied, "Sure, call it guesswork, but I can tell you this—to get ahead of the Talbots you not only have to outshoot them, but to outguess them, as well! They'll try to buy Mary's farm now. They have to have it, Len."

Len Rathburn showed some excitement. "I wish I could git out of this thing. I'd be hangin' a Talbot hide over the fireplace." He settled down, lips quivering. "Mary, you gonna sell to them?"

"No," said Mary simply but with determination.

Len leaned back, breathing deeply. Squaw watched, unmindful that the coffee pot had tipped and was streaming on to the floor. Jim noticed the stubborn set of the girl's face.

"I sell to nobody under suspicion of killing my father."

Jim asked, "Will you sell to us?"

She swung her glance up to him. For a moment her eyes held his. But her eyes were not soft and yielding, as he had hoped.

"I will sell to nobody, Jim Rathburn. I've had a terrible shock, but I'm getting over it and I'm determined. I'll rebuild that place if it takes all my life. Until I can find a way to do it I'll squat on it until something turns up that will give me a chance. My father loved that place. He had been all over the world, and in the end that was where he had wanted to live and die. Well, he died there, and as his daughter I'm going to fight for what was his, for the land where he is going to be buried."

There was a silence. Squaw discovered that she had been pouring coffee on the floor instead of into one of the cups, and Len's knuckles were white from where he had gripped the arms of his wheel chair.

Jim simply said, "Well spoken, Mary. It hardly seems possible that the Talbots would move against you, but you can never tell with that ruthless pair. Len will keep an eye on you and there is no reason why you shouldn't stay on here until the weather breaks. You must decide for yourself, but you're sure welcome to stay, Mary."

"We want you," Squaw said.

"Thanks. But I have to get into Branding Iron to make arrangements for the funeral and I should go there right away."

Jim said, "I'll drive you in, Mary. I'm doin' no good here. I'm just wearing out the floor."

"Take the bobsled," Len suggested.

"Flip and Dan are a couple of stout horses and they'll get you through."

Jim went outside to get one of the hands to harness the team, pulling on his sheepskin coat as he went. The storm hit him with savage ferocity as he crossed over the porch. While he was away Squaw fixed Mary up with some warm clothing, and by the time Jim returned with the bobsled the girl was ready and waiting to go.

Jim helped her into a seat and then tucked a blanket round her legs. She smiled at him and said, "Gosh, but it's cold."

Squaw waddled out, carrying a Winchester rifle and a box of cartridges. "Len he say maybe you want this, too, son," she explained.

Jim thanked her and put the rifle at their feet, laying it crosswise with the wagon-box. Then he turned the team and they trotted towards a town they could not see because of the snowfall.

Flip was a big grey and Dan a fine, strong bay and both horses knew the road, even if they could not see it. As they jogged along the bobsled runners cut into the deep snow and tossed it aside. The journey led through fairly deep drifts, but the horses kept going and ploughed their way through.

Jim's free hand slipped under the blanket over their laps and he found Mary's gloved hand. He held it in his own.

"You're a swell girl," he told her.

"Thanks, Jim."

His hand tightened on hers. "Jus' be brave and strong, Mary. Although things are tough now everything will work out right in the end."

He told her about the death of his father and brother down on the Red River in Texas, but not about how he had avenged their murders. He reckoned it was little use to talk about guns just then. The girl had known enough trouble of her own this last few days.

Jim kept hold of her hand and would have liked to have taken her in his arms and kissed and caressed her, but it wasn't the time to reveal his feelings in this way.

They talked about the Talbots, and the drift fence the brothers had set their hearts upon, and time passed swiftly, so it seemed. Just outside of Branding Iron they sighted another bobsled. Mary said it belonged to the owner of the hardware store, and so it appeared, for it was heavily loaded with barbed wire.

Jim pulled up the horses and asked, "Some more farmers movin' in?"

The old driver shook his head. "Goin' out to your friends, the Talbots. They aim to start diggin' post holes and stringing wire."

Jim nodded. "Understand they need some deeds yet?"

"Done got them on the last stage. Yep, stage got through, an' it had the deeds. Now the Talbots got all the land they need 'cept that owned by Miss Jones here. That is unless you've sold already."

"I haven't sold," replied Mary. "And what is more, I won't."

The old man nodded and Jim called on

the horses to move before anything further could be said.

They drove on.

"You didn't let me finish what I had to say," Mary accused him.

"No use tipping your hand before you have to," answered the escort.

Now they could see the rimrock that marked the top of the high south benchlands. The snow had stopped falling. The landscape glistened before them, cold and perfectly, dazzling white.

None of the rimrock's gigantic boulders could be seen, even though many of them towered upwards for thirty feet or more. Jim peered at the scene, looking for some trace, however faint, of the rimrock trail. None showed.

Gullies and canyons were banked with deep snow. No cow would ever come off the rimrock in those conditions, nor could man or horse hope to get up there. There was a hidden challenge, Jim felt, white and stirring, yet holding death in its white serenity. Anger stirred Jim, but he couldn't blot out the grim reality of the situation.

"Well, here we are in town," said Mary breaking through to him.

Jim continued to watch the rimrock. It made him feel a prisoner—a captive bound by this great snowbound land.

Nature had handcuffed him.

13

Blizzard Herd

BROKEN NOSE, the Sioux, knew how fast the weather could change. Jim and Mary had only been away from the cow camp a few minutes when he ordered, "Get 'em movin'! Fast, too."

Bronc Thomas rode close, face pale with cold.

"What's the rush, Injun? These cattle is tired."

"Move 'em, fast." The Sioux made a sign in the sign-language. "Snow come, then blizzard."

"Blizzard! Hell, this ain't winter time —this is middle of the fall. All the same that wind is mighty cold."

"Blizzard he come, Bronc."

Bronc Thomas waved his arm to his riders. "Get 'em movin', men, an' push 'em toward the rimrock! We get locked upon this mesa an' it'll be spring afore we get down!"

There in the dawn, Texas men started Texas cattle moving. Bronc Thomas and the other Bucking Horse cowboys had run into blizzards in Texas, but this Montana blizzard was something new. The world turned into a solid blanket of white snow.

Bull whips and lariats popped, as slowly the cattle moved, heads down into the storm. But, at the most, they never got three miles off the bed ground. Bronc Thomas rode to where Broken Nose rode.

"I come from the lead, Sioux. They won't move. They're turnin' with thet wind. We got to keep from driftin' or we'll lose them. How far to the rimrock trail down into Milk River valley?"

The old Sioux looked about him for landmarks. But the snow had cut visibility. "Long ways yet. We get the trail snowed in an' we have to stay here. No can take cows down on Milk River."

Bronc Thomas cursed as only a trailman can. "Everythin' has gone wrong. Now thet boss of mine has even run off with a stray female. Is thet rimrock trail the only trail down, Broken Nose?"

"Larb Crick trail. Twenty miles to west. But snow there too, I think."

"How far west?"

"Over twenty mile west."

Bronc cursed again. "Never get around to it if it keeps on snowin'. What do we do with the cattle now? They won't go into the blizzard. They want to drift."

"Keep 'em bunched thick."

A cowboy loped up, bullwhip coiled. "They're really turnin' on us now, Bronc. They cain't wade into thet wind."

Bronc Thomas snapped sullenly. "Get behind them, Sulky. Don't try to drive them. Broken Nose says only thing to do is keep them from driftin'."

Bronc turned his horse, said, "I'll spread the word to the boys. Broken Nose, whether you like it or not, you're trailboss here—you know this kentry, I don't."

He loped off. Within a few feet, the

storm hid him. Cattle were beginning to drift. They were humped-up, rumps to the blizzard, tired and hungry. They bawled with plaintive loneliness. Bronc Thomas turned them and cursed the world in general. He wished Jim Rathburn had stayed to help.

One day from winter graze, and they had to run into a blizzard.

They were in a rather flat country, broken only by a few coulees and draws. The big thing, Bronc reasoned, was to keep the cattle out of the low-lying spots. Once they got in a coulee the snow would suffocate them. A rider came out of the storm, head down to the wind.

"Bronc," he called.

"Over here, Curly."

Curly panted, "We can't haze them ahead, Bronc. They turn and break on us. What do we do in a case like this?"

"The Sioux says bunch them on a level spot and hold them there. Keep them from driftin' whatever happens. They'll go to hell and gone with this storm pushin' 'em, Curly."

"The Indian should know," Curly replied. "I sure don't. We might lose this herd, after trailin' all this way . . . Be tough on Jim."

"Spread the word to the boys. Stay within shoutin' range of each other. We got to pull through and save as many of the cows as we can. Play a close hand, Curly."

Curly said, "Slim's over thisaway," and loped into the storm, drifting out of sight almost instantly. The storm seemed to reach out and grab him. One moment he was with Bronc Thomas, the next moment he was gone. No hoof beats, not a sound. It was uncanny. Bronc felt the pull of unknown forces and was almost scared, but the feeling didn't stay long with him.

He ran into other riders; they built a barrier and stopped the cattle, riding backwards and forwards and fighting the elements. The men had to beat the cattle with anything they could find to stop them drifting. Luckily the cattle were so tired that less and less they became prone to stray. They wanted to lie down perhaps to die.

Gradually the herd settled down, becoming a packed unit. They stood with their rumps to the wind and snow. Those on the outside had it the worst, for they were without the warmth of each other, and they dropped their heads hopelessly.

Broken Nose said, "We hold them. But they have no hay."

One of the hands with a wry smile suggested they ought to train a flock of eagles to fly in a few bales of hay. It was good that somebody had a joke left in him. There was no sun, only snow that fell endlessly in the grey light and held them in captivity.

Somewhere there were cities, full of life, rivers that flowed, and flowers that bloomed, but that was another part of the world. Here they were cut off from civilisation and, so it seemed, from the past and the future. The only thought among them was to keep alive and try and save the cows. Nothing else counted.

"Cattle," said a cowboy with a world of meaning, "Cattle."

"Without cattle," said Bronc "there would be no cowboys and without cattle there'd be no Texas, nor Montana for that matter."

"Listen to Bronc," said another "Here we are ready and likely to die in a blizzard and he starts talking like from a book."

"Who the 'ell wants to hear about cattle or Texas," asked another voice. "How about Houston, Bronc? Think them purty girls still walk the streets down there, sunbonnets tilted?"

"Can it." Texas stormed in mock anger. "Always remindin' a man of somethin' warm and good."

"Some women ain't that good," another rider said. "Should've met my first wife—hell on shoe leather she was."

To add to their troubles they were short on camp supplies and the cook had to start in and ration flour and other stuff. They shot one of their fattest beeves, but he had been too long on the trail to be really appetising.

Another problem was the lack of fuel and they had to dig down deep to get at the roots of the sage-brush. One man had a watch and by this they lived and marked the passing of the hours. When daylight came the sky was a little brighter, but really there was little difference between night and day.

There was always the thick, swirling snow and within a couple of days about three hundred cattle had frozen to death. The snow covered their icy bodies. The men tried to guess the temperature, but it was too cold to even think about it.

As cattle sank to their knees and heeled over to die Bronc almost wept, for cattle were his life, and he felt that life was being dragged out of him.

He thought of Jim Rathburn down in the valley and guessed how much raw anxiety and worry he would be enduring. If the storm kept on for a week the Texas part of the Bucking Horse herd would be wiped out. Cowpunchers cut down sage brush and willows and fed them to their broncs, but the animals were weak and many had developed a cough that boded no good.

Time ran on and on and Bronc found himself praying for a let-up from the cruel weather. But the blizzards continued and more cattle sank to the ground never to rise again. Four days went by in this way and on the fifth another hundred head of the Bucking Horse stock succumbed. The men, gaunt and unshaven suffered badly with frost-bite and exhaustion.

Came the sixth and the cook announced that all flour and staples had gone and that there was only a bit of beef left. But for once the sun was out and it made the gleaming snow hard and hurtful on the eyes, like coming out of a cavern into sudden light.

The next day, however, when Bronc Thomas crawled painfully out of his blankets, there was surprise on the frost-bitten, unshaven face of the old Texas trail driver.

"It's warm," he yelled frantically, "the storm is over."

The men stood together and watched as

the wind came in and they marvelled at what they saw. They had never before witnessed a Chinook, the *foehn* wind. From the far distant Rocky Mountains it came, a slow, hot wind. It was like somebody opening a furnace door.

"What is it?" someone asked.

The Sioux replied, "It is the Chinook wind. He cut the snow like a knife and soon all will be water."

"Thank God," his questioner replied.

Already cattle were showing renewed life. The wind was warming them and they sensed, indeed they knew that their agonising trial was over. Although the warmth spread slowly, by evening the snow was on the move, and the ground in some places began to show a few bare spots. The starving cattle grazed dry grass to its roots. They tore into willows and choke-cherry bushes and stripped them to the ground.

Life began to return to them and they bawled and horned each other.

There was a moon that night.

When dawn came, a rider came over

the ridge, gaunt and near to exhaustion. Bronc saw him first and hollered out as he rode over to Jim Rathburn.

"Jim, you made it—up the rimrock trail, too!"

Jim dismounted, saying, "My horse is done for. I started out with pack-horse and supplies. He's back there somewhere in the snow. He went off a ledge and was killed.

"We'll get the supplies off him. A couple of the boys can work on that. Man, we've had a rough time—if it hadn't been for Broken Nose we'd've all died of cold."

Riders, astraddle woe-begone horses, came around them, and Broken Nose, the Sioux, rubbed his jaw, grinning at Jim. Plenty of questions were asked and three men left to search for the pack-horse.

Jim said, "We lost a bunch, eh?"

"About three hundred," Bronc said.

By this time the ground was almost bare of snow. Water stood in pools. Jim looked at the Sioux.

"Will this water bring some grass, or is it too late in the year?"

"It brings grass, Jim. Not a lot, like the spring rains, but it help a lot for this winter when more snow come."

"A tough range," Bronc Thomas said.

Jim looked at the sky. Blue as Texas bluebonnets, serene, with no clouds. The wind was warm and good. His cattle were grazing, although graze was slim.

"But a good land," he said. "As good, if not better, than Texas. Tomorrow we move cattle down the rimrock trail, men."

"Down on Milk River," Broken Nose intoned.

14

Drift Fence

BOWIE TALBOT leaned from his saddle. He wore a long sheepskin coat and overshoes covered his feet.

His gunbelt was strapped outside of his overcoat and two black Colts glistened in the light reflected from the melting snowbanks.

"How is it comin', Ole?"

The big Swede grinned. He had no need for an overcoat. Sweat was on his wide ugly face. He had been digging post holes in the rocky soil despite the snow.

"They're hard to dig, Bowie," he answered.

Bowie straightened in the saddle, shifting his weight to the stirrups. He looked at the men working on the fence. They had been at the job for two days. A halt had had to be called when the storm was at its height, but now progress had been resumed, although foothold was slippery.

Ole looked at the fence that was going up and said, "She have the zig-zag in her, Bowie. But it makes no difference, does it?"

"The wire is on our deeded land," the Heart Nine man said. "A few bends in it will only catch more Buckin' Horse cows when the storms drive them against it this winter."

"Wish the fence had been up before the present blow. Some Buckin' Horse cattle are on our range already."

Bowie smiled, eyes narrowed. "Good, Ole. We'll fence them on our side and make the owners come after them. That might be something to look forward to."

"Sure might, Bowie."

Bowie turned his bronc. "Keep up the good work, men," he said as he rode away. Luck, he reckoned, had dealt him a good hand. The stray cattle from Bucking Horse would come in useful. The owners would most certainly want them back, and it was just the kind of situation that might force the Rathburns, uncle and nephew, into open warfare, which would suit the book of Bowie and his brother very nicely. It was just what they wanted.

It turned out that many Bucking Horse cows had drifted onto their range. The further Bowie rode, and the more cattle he saw, the greater became his elation. About two thousand of Len Rathburn's stock, he figured, had drifted east with the storm. They would be behind the fence when it was completed.

Len could come after his stock, through the fence, but that would be the incident to start the Milk River war, Bowie figured. He rode back to where a crew was stringing wire to diamond-willow posts.

"String like hell, boys," he encouraged. "We got about two thousand of Len's cattle to play with."

"We need more men," said Ole. "Crew is too small."

"I'll send help from town. Bunch of

loafin' cowboys around the saloons. They've been laid off for the winter."

"They might not like the idea of a gunfight," advised Ole.

Bowie grinned. "I'll give them a spiel," he said as he left for Branding Iron. He had sent Knife over to the Jones place to talk to Mary, and he wondered how he was making out.

When Knife Talbot had ridden into the yard of the Jones' farm, Mary had been doing some washing, bending over a tub set on a bench in the yard. Because of this she had not heard him ride in, and she turned in surprise at his voice.

"Howdy, Miss Mary."

"Oh, hello!"

She straightened, and began to dry her hands on the apron she wore. She was bareheaded, and her red hair glistened in the Montana sun.

"You—you scared me, Mr. Talbot."

Knife did not like the title. He remembered the day in the cabin when he had tried to hold her.

"Knife is the name, Mary."

Mary said, “My pup left me again. I guess he must have returned to the Bucking Horse ranch. He likes to play with the dogs over there.”

“You found him—after the fire?”

“Yes.”

Knife said, slowly, “Maybe he followed one of the Buckin’ Horse men back to the ranch, after the fire.”

Mary said, “The Rathburns didn’t set fire to my place, nor did they kill my father. I’m sure of that.”

Knife decided to change the subject. He was on dangerous ground. “You used to kinda like me,” he said, looking at her.

She saw from the light in his eyes that she was in for trouble. She had played up to him deliberately that day in order to make things easier for her father, maybe this man had killed him? The thought roused her, but she knew it was safer to temporise.

“I still—like you, a little.”

He came closer. “Couldn’t you make it not a little, but a lot?”

She quickly changed the subject. "Why did you come over here, Knife?"

"To see you, Mary."

"You had other business, too."

His eyes bored into hers. "Yes, about sellin' out to me an' Bowie. You ain't got no call to run this farm alone, honey."

"I don't care to sell."

"You've said that afore, honey. But you're jus' a little girl—you can't farm an' build fence with them little hands."

He tried to grab "them little hands." But Mary anticipated the move, and "them little hands" went behind her back very quickly.

"Mr. Talbot, I want nothing to do with you. Not one single thing, business or otherwise! I want you to ride off this farm and stay off, and don't come back, please!"

He grabbed her. The move was too fast for her and she was in his arms. She heard his coarse, animal breathing and she got the smell of him, his unwashed body, of tobacco, of whisky on his breath. She felt him push against her, and fear arose in her, so that she was near to helpless terror.

She was alone on the farm, miles from the closest neighbour. He was husky and strong, hungry for her. These thoughts added to her fright. Yet she managed to keep her voice steady as she looked up at him, limp in his grip, and with her hands at her sides.

"Let me go Knife, please let me go."

He tried to kiss her, but somehow she evaded his fumbling attempt, and instead, his lips brushed her cheek. The contact galvanised Knife into a frenzied fervour and Mary could see that he was quickly losing all sense of restraint.

The thought that a man, who had probably slain her father, was trying to make love to her drove Mary nearly frantic, but fear, deadly fear, was uppermost in her mind. As she struggled to release herself she wondered if Knife might not go berserk and, in his rage, kill her if she refused to surrender. Somehow she had to get away from him and his animal passion.

"Let-me-go!"

"You little devil. You she-devil. I'll master you and then. . . ." Mary got her right hand free and promptly slapped Knife across the face. Mary read what was in his eyes and, unable to hit him again as he crushed her to him, she began to kick and scream.

"I don't want you. I've got a good man, a real man, and when he hears of this he'll kill you, Knife Talbot," she gasped.

As he strained her to him, and she felt her strength sapping, he gloated, "You're at the end of the your little struggle and nobody's going to kill me."

Mary felt limpness and defeat stealing over her and she gasped, "My man will. Jim Rathburn will make you pay for this."

No sooner had she spoken however than she saw someone standing behind Knife, who had suddenly gone rigid. Faintly she heard a voice say, "I've got a gun in your back, you swine. Let go of her if you know what's good for you."

Talbot stood there as if turned to stone.

Only his lips twitched and slowly he released Mary.

White of face and trembling Mary stepped back and said, "Thank God you came, Jim. Watch him."

"Turn round Talbot."

Talbot did so, hands shoulder high only to look down at the broom handle he had been bluffed into thinking was a gun. Before he could recover Jim clipped a right on his jaw, knocking him back. Another swift punch knocked him over and as he rolled in the mud before coming up in a crouching position. "I'll kill you Rathburn," he said.

Knife dived for his gun, but Jim hit him once more, this time with the broom handle. It whipped in and Knife went down and lost his gun at the same time. Before Knife could recover it Mary had picked it up.

"What do you aim to do?" she asked him.

"I'm not going to hurt my knuckles belting him. I'm going to pistol whip him."

Although Talbot was hurt he had still to be reckoned with, particularly when he released a punch that put Jim on the ground. Jim rolled over and came up with his gun in his hand with which he began to flay his opponent.

Knife was driven back, step by step and, although he resisted desperately, he failed to ward off the blows from the gun in Jim's hand and soon blood was pouring from his head and face. He had to take a tremendous beating however before he broke and collapsed at last, out to the world.

Jim, who had taken plenty too, spat blood before he turned to Mary to ask her if she was all right.

"Yes," she answered, "but it was a near thing. I was almost exhausted and at his mercy. How did you manage to ride in just in time?"

"Came over to tell you we're movin' cattle off the rimrock. Want you along, Mary."

"I'll go—What about him?"

"We'll soon fix him," said Jim as he

led Talbot's horse over and then hoisted the unconscious man over the saddle, jackknifing him across the kak. Then, tying his hands and feet to the cinch, he ran the rope under the bronc and tied the reins around the saddlehorn. When Jim whipped the bronc across the back with the broom handle the animal broken into a lope with Knife bouncing in the saddle. The horse went over the hill and out of sight.

Jim washed his face in the horse trough and wiped himself with a towel Mary brought to him. She was very womanly and she looked prettier than ever.

"How do I look, Miss Jones?"

"Not as bad as you did after the fight in the hotel."

"You sure read the riot act to me that night. Redhead, I heard every word you told Talbot, and I'm holdin' you to them!"

Her eyes met his. "I don't—understand."

He was holding her now. "Oh, yes, you do, young woman. You told Talbot you already had found your man, and that his name was Jim Rathburn."

"You weren't supposed to hear. I never knew you were around, otherwise I wouldn't have said it."

"Are you sure of that?"

"Of course I'm sure."

By this time, his arms had, somehow, gotten around her. They were pulling her close to him. Her eyes met his.

"Jim, I'm not telling—the truth."

"I know that." His eyes danced. "I haven't kissed a woman for ages. I wonder if I can try now, seein' she is willin'?"

"No one's stopping you."

When they broke she said, "You did a good job of that. Let's try it again. . . ."

Their second kiss lasted longer. She stepped back at last and said, "Let's take cattle off the rimrock, Jim."

"Together," he said happily.

15

Trail to Milk River

CATTLE were on the move—through mud and banks of snow. Cows that were bony and tired and had somehow miraculously survived the blizzards and lived. They were bound for the rimrock trail that led down into Milk River valley.

Behind lay the outer cattle that had come over a thousand miles to meet death in Montana. They lay in coulees and gullies, among buck brush and choke-cherry bushes, Bucking Horse cows that would never again be on the hoof.

Broken Nose, the Sioux, rode the point. They came to the rimrock trail that led down, twisting and bending through rocks, across lava ridges. Below them lay the broad valley. The Indian waved his hand. "Drift fence goin' in," he explained.

They could see the Heart Nine fencers, working to the north side of the valley. Digging post holes, tamping down, stringing the single strand of wire which heralded death here in northern Montana. The Sioux turned and looked at the weary cattle and said to Bronc Thomas, "I know this trail. No push the cattle. Let 'em go like they want, slow."

"You're the trail boss on this run, Sioux," said Bronc.

That was how it went, slow and sure. The ledge they reached became the first downthrust of the trail and the lead cows halted. Ropes were used to prod them on, and saddle-horses turned them. One cow gingerly started downward with braced hoofs. She slipped and almost fell but retained her hold. Others followed behind.

Broken Nose stood on oxbows and made the cattle walk. If they once piled up on each other disaster would ensue, and there would be no way to halt the slaughter.

Along this trail buffalo had once moved, but their day was over for history had turned its pages and many things that had once been were now no longer. The Indian, watchful and silent, rode with his body braced against the fork of the saddle. His horse stepped slowly, forelegs stiff and hind legs braced. He was shod well and, although sure-footed, knew that danger faced him.

A bull bellowed as he slid off the narrow trail. He slid down but recovered, got himself upright and moved slowly along the hill, working his way back to trail.

Broken Nose rubbed his jaw. His skin was peeling from too much exposure to cold and wind.

They inched downwards—men, horses, cattle. At last Sioux reached the level ground with the lead cow directly behind him. He reined to one side to allow her to get by. Others followed and began to graze down in the basin, free of danger at last.

Broken Nose looked at the short grass and then at the sky, his big eyes rolling in his dark face. Not a cloud in sight. A cowman depends on grass and knows the value of rain. Just then a man rode out of the coulee and the Sioux spotted him.

"Len all by hisself," he noted.

Len Rathburn was clean shaven but his skin was loose and pale. "I sneaked out," he said by way of explanation. "Rode out to see how a poor cowdog earns his bacon an' beans."

"Squaw, she watch you?"

"I snuck out, I tell you."

"Squaw, she break her voice, hollerin'."

"Let her holler. I'm not in good shape, but I'm puttin' on some flesh. But never mind about me where's that worthless nephew of mine?"

"He with girl somewhere."

Len looked at his old friend. "You got a face like rawhide. You mean to say Jim is out chasin' women at a time like this?"

"He go after redhead."

"Two redheads together. Bet the kids'll all be redheads. Wish I had a bottle and we'd drink to them."

"Wish we had bottle, we'd jus' drink!"

Len Rathburn moved his weight on his stirrups. "Good to be out on a hoss again. Man is no 'count without a hoss. He can get by without a woman but not without a bronc. They're runnin' bobwire, Injun."

Broken Nose said, "Our cows drift east in snow storm?"

Len looked at him and nodded.

"How many head, you think."

"The storm hit them hard. Pushed about two thousan' or so into the east end of the basin. They run thet drift fence between us an' them an' we cut it from here to gundy, Injun!"

"Legal, hell. Only a Winchester an' a short-gun is legal here. They know thet an' so does Sheriff Harden."

Broken Nose nodded. "Winchesters," he said. "Here comes two riders now, Len."

Len looked at them coming over a hill

and said, "He'll be surprised, Broken Nose. She's a likely-looking filly, thet girl. She rides a saddle like she was raised to one."

Jim looked at his uncle and then at Broken Nose. "Do ghosts ride?" he asked.

"In the flesh," Len said.

Jim said, "Good to see you on a horse, though I hate to compliment an ol' rawhider like you. Who helped you get on thet ol' plug?"

"Did it on my lonesome."

Jim was earnest as he said, "You sure you're not rushin' things, Len?"

Len Rathburn shook his grizzled head. "I'm not rushin' a thing. But them Talbots is when they string thet drift fence wire. They're rushin' into hell, if you'll pardon my French, Miss Jones."

Broken Nose said, "You get in fight again, Jim?"

Jim told him of the fight with Knife Talbot. He and Mary had agreed to keep the reason for it to themselves. He just said that Knife had jumped him and that he had in turn whipped the Heart Nine man, tied him to his bronc, and sent him towards the Heart Nine ranch.

"His brother Bowie—he be su'prised," the Sioux said slowly. "Like to see his face when the horse come in, Knife tied to him."

Jim turned his bronc. "We got cattle to move. They're jammin' up in front of the hill. Len, they say your cows drifted, eh?"

"They'll be behind thet drift fence."

Jim turned his horse. "They still can't string wire across Mary's land. We can round up an' chase them back across her land."

"No dice, Jim."

Jim looked at his uncle. "I can't blame you. You settled here and it is open range. We cut the fence, then, and drive our cows whenever we want, and where we want?"

"We cut the fence."

Broken Nose rubbed his jaw. "War," he said.

Len Rathburn snapped, "Sure, it's

war. And war is still hell, no matter how they boost it up to a man! I've stood enough. I pack one of their bullets in my brisket."

Mary looked at Jim, her face pale. Jim didn't feel too good, either. A bullet made all men the same size.

Jim made a signal to her, and she moved away and rode with him. The cattle were hungry and there was some dried tall buffalo grass in this coulee and they wanted to graze. That made the cattle coming down block the trail. Jim and Mary moved them down.

Mary said, "I'll never sell my land!"

Jim nodded, "And you won't live there alone, either. Your next home will be built by me, either here in Milk River valley or in Canada."

"What about my place?"

Jim's jaw became grim. "You don't go back there alone. Bronc an' me we stay there from now on. Maybe one or two of my men, too."

"Why don't you make it your camp for

the winter? You could live in the toolshed until we build another house."

Jim said, "I'll talk it over with Bronc."

"They'll never run wire across my land," she said. "I'll die first, Jim. So help me I will . . . for Dad. Jim, I've just found you, and what if I lost you? Jim, keep me from thinking about losing you, please!"

They were in a coulee and hidden. Jim rode close and put his arm around her and their broncs stood shoulder to shoulder. The aroma of her hair was in his nostrils.

"Honey, just have faith, please."

Her eyes had tears, as he kissed her slowly. They were very much in love, very much alone, very dependent upon each other.

16

Rifle Riders

THEY were strong and well-kept hands. The owner of them did no physical work. Now the owner preferred looking at them rather than at Bowie Talbot. Linklatter said, "So Knife rode over to see Mary Jones, eh? He's gone for that woman, Bowie."

Bowie Talbot stood beside the window and answered: "A woman ain't got no call to run a farm alone in this wild country. Thet girl should be taken off thet homestead for her own good. Hope Knife can make her see the light."

Linklatter said, "How about the Buckin' Horse herd—the Texas herd? Once you said we was going to stampede it. That plan still hold?"

Bowie Talbot did not turn. Linklatter watched the weather-roughed side of the

Heart Nine man's face. He saw a tight little smile move the skin.

"You cain't stampede cattle thet are so weak in the pins they cain't run, Linklatter."

A man and a woman came out of the store and went past the office, chatting as they carried home their groceries. Across the street three Heart Nine broncs stood at the hitchrack as their riders drank inside. A dog ambled along, nose down, looking for grub.

"Hell of a lookin' town," Bowie said.

Unrest was gnawing at him. He was not a man of streets, of saloons, of stores—but a man of saddle leather, of wide and untrampled lands, of Winchesters and Colts. There was an enemy to be destroyed, and this tasked called to him. He had tried once, but the bullets had failed to kill, and Len Rathburn still lived. So too did Jim, Len's nephew, an even more formidable enemy. He remembered the gun fight between Jim and the man who tried to kill him. Jim Rathburn's gun had talked to some purpose that day. After the flurry of words had come the gun play and Bowie still recollected Jim's fast action.

As Linklatter watched him he saw the big right hand of Bowie Talbot go to his head, and the fingers explore through the thick hair. Stitches were there that had to be sewn in when Rathburn had knocked him out with all the town looking on.

Bowie knew that he could never rest content until these stitches, and the affront that had been done to him had been paid for, and he would never settle for less than Jim Rathburn's life and the more violently it was snuffed out the better.

Actually Jim was in Linklatter's thoughts too. He was well aware of the hatred the Talbots felt for Len's nephew and he shared it too, but for a different reason. He had allowed himself to be drawn into a quarrel with Jim Rathburn, which wasn't at all smart and then when Rathburn had left he (Linklatter) had boasted that sooner or later he would kill him. That wasn't particularly smart either. He ought to have kept his nose out of it and let the Talbots and Rathburn settle their own differences. If they wiped each other out the world would certainly be a safer place for Martin Linklatter.

Just then, Monte, one of the Heart Nine riders looked in and Bowie snarled, "What in hell do you want?"

Monte gave him a surprised glance and then smiled. "You're as touchy as a bear with a thorn festerin' in his paw," he said. "Just dropped in to see what was new in the deal, boss."

"Get over to the saloon, get a drink and sit tight. I'll know where you are if I want you."

Monte's grin widened. "That sounds good to me," he replied. He left, chaps swishing, rowels talking. Bowie watched him cross the street, walking with the bowlegged gait of a horseman on foot.

Martin Linklatter was still thinking of his problems. He was tired of them and the whole set-up and wanted to get out of Milk River valley, whole, and with all the money that had come his way.

"How about the Jones deed, Martin?" Bowie asked suddenly.

Linklatter didn't answer at once, but finally said, "There might be a way to break it. But I'm not attorney enough to determine that for certain. The awkward part is that Lester Jones had the homestead entry made out in his daughter's name, too. Had it been in his name only —and with him now dead—we would have stood a better chance."

Linklatter got to his feet. "There might be some way to muscle in and break the entry. I've got a lawyer working on it, but it'll be a slow job."

"We can't wait," said Bowie tersely.

"There's nothing further that can be done yet."

Suddenly Bowie's jaw hardened, muscles going taut. He was watching something that Linklatter could not see from where he was standing. The locator saw Bowie's mouth open slightly.

"What in the name of?"

Bowie's startled exclamation drew Linklatter over to the window in a few strides. He saw that a horse had entered the street carrying a bound man across the saddle.

Linklatter ejaculated, "That's Knife, sure as eggs!"

But Bowie was already scuttling out of the room. Linklatter followed. When Bowie and the land locator reached Knife he had already been untied, and was on one knee rubbing his cut and bruised wrists. Bowie gave the saddle a quick look, saw that there was no blood on it, and then turned his attention to his crouching brother.

"That's a new way to come into town," he said drily.

Knife Talbot massaged his wrists. He did not look up. "Close your ugly mouth!" he snarled.

Knife was bareheaded. Blood had matted in his thick hair. Bowie Talbot jerked his brother to his feet. He saw a broken, bloody face, cuts across the nose. He pushed him ahead, and Knife lurched towards Linklatter's office.

"Not a word, Knife, until we get alone!

Linklatter go after the doc, and make it snappy."

A man asked, "What happened?"

Bowie promptly punched him in the face, and he staggered away under the impact of the blow.

"I only asked you a question," he remonstrated.

"I only socked you in the mush, too," Bowie gritted. "You ol' gossips ought to learn some day to keep your traps shut." He turned to Knife and said, "Get along."

"Take it easy with your blasted orders."

"Get movin'."

Knife was not too steady on his feet. They got to the door of the land locator's office and Bowie gave his brother a hard shove. Knife staggered inside, and then keeled over onto the floor.

As he rolled over he looked up at his brother, who stood wide-legged in the doorway. Knife's lips moved, and it was the gesture of a sick and cornered animal. At first he was unable to speak but at last he managed to gasp, "Don't shove me aroun'! I'm goin' to get Rathburn for what he's done to me today."

"You've said all that before. So it was him, eh? Caught you at the Jones' spread and then laid the gun barrel on you!"

Bowie stepped forward, his face dark with rage as he kicked out at his brother. Knife scrambled out of the way and got to his feet up against the wall.

"So you let him use a gun barrel on you."

"His short-gun . . . an' a broom handle."

"A—*broom handle!*"

Bowie's eyes were wild with rage now. He kicked Knife in the belly, doubling him up. Bowie would have booted him again but the door opened and Linklatter and the doctor came in. Bowie said, "There's your patient, doc."

The doc got Knife Talbot into a chair and examined him. Bowie watched, eyes narrowed; he remembered things—the townspeople had laughed at Knife Talbot and, because they had derided his brother, they had indirectly made fun of him, too.

Martin Linklatter stood by. He was thinking that this would drive the Talbots openly against the Bucking Horse brand. He did not want to be caught in the middle.

The doc said, "Some more sewing to do."

A woman came in to lend a hand and when the doctor said he would need some hot water Linklatter started a fire in the heater.

Before the doctor left Harden came in and asked what happened. Reluctantly Bowie said, "He tangled with one of the Buckin' Horse men."

"Which one?"

"That's our business," Bowie answered.

Sheriff Harden continued to chew on a plug of tobacco, but it was obvious that he was angered.

"Bowie," he warned, "don't rub this lawman's fur the wrong way. You'll be sorry if you do."

Bowie answered, "You're a Buckin' Horse man, Harden. Everybody on the range knows that Rathburn votes got you into office and that they keep you there."

When Harden again warned Bowie to keep a bridle on his tongue the Heart Nine man decided that the time had come for a showdown.

"We know whose side you're on in this trouble," he sneered. "But we've counted you out of this picture, lock, stock and barrel."

"I carry the badge," Harden reminded him.

Bowie laughed harshly. "Carry it to your grave, Harden, if it pleases you. This is a big range and the nights are dark. You're out of this so far as the Heart Nine is concerned."

Harden lifted his sunken, lonely eyes and looked around before replying. At last he said, "You might count me out, Bowie," he said, "but that doesn't concern me. I still tote the badge and draw county pay."

"You savvy all right what I've just told you. We both know where we stand, eh?"

Harden stared at Bowie but without replying he turned on his heel and went out.

Bowie through the window watched the sheriff stalk down the street and his lips, as Linklatter saw, curled into a slow smile.

"You certainly told him, Bowie," his brother said.

In answer Bowie pulled out a .45 and looked at it. "If he crosses us," he replied, "this gun kills him."

There was silence for a few seconds until Knife suddenly said, "Jeez, I feel like hell."

"I'll bet you do," said Linklatter with his eyes still on Bowie's gun.

Bowie fondled it like a friend.

17

Range Camp

THE snow was almost gone. Only in coulees and behind sagebrush was there any trace of it. The wagon inched along the road, team braced against collars. It carried wire and staples and the heaviness of the load caused the wheels to sink deep into the mud.

Jim Rathburn, sitting his horse in the high brush of a coulee, saw the wagon coming and shook down his lasso. From the corner of his mouth he said, "This is it, Bronc. This is one load that doesn't reach the Heart Nine outfit. Cover me with your rifle."

Bronc was in the brush, rifle across his lap. Behind him stood his horse, reins trailing. "I'll pertect you, Jim," he assured Rathburn.

Jim rode out, horse sliding in the mud.

He shouted, "Hello, there, pull up!" The driver of the wagon tied his reins around the brake handle and reached down for the rifle which he had next to him on the seat he was using. Just then Bronc fired and the bullet sang dangerously close. The driver forgot about his own rifle and reached for the sky.

"Don't get smart," Jim said, "otherwise you may get killed."

He was a short, stocky little man whom Jim had seen around the town. "What's the deal Rathburn?" he asked.

"This load ain't reachin' the drift fence. Get off the seat, climb down an' unhook your team and then take them to the Heart Nine if you want to."

The driver did as he was ordered, but still had another question to ask. "What do you aim to do?" he enquired.

Jim answered, "That's something you'll find out later. Now get goin' with the horses. We don't mind killin' someone who asks for it, but killin' innocent animal is another deal."

Jim relieved the man of his pistol,

threw it into the brush and then told him to beat it for the Heart Nine.

"Not me," he answered with a crooked smile.

"And why not?"

"Bowie's wild enough as it is. He'd handle me worse than he did Knife when he come into town yesterday."

"Treated his little brother rough, eh?"

"I'll say he did."

Jim had a fair idea why Bowie had cut up rough, but deemed the conversation had gone on long enough and said brusquely, "Now get that team a-movin' an' move fast!"

The driver hurriedly got a leg on the horse on the offside, and rode away with tug chains jangling. As Jim reached for the rifle the driver had left behind, and tossed it into the brush in a wide arc, Bronc rode down.

"That driver's done drifted hell for leather round the bend, Jim. Hope this powder deal works okay."

Jim nodded, and when he laid a stick of dynamite on the reach of the wagon

Bronc quickly retreated. Jim used plenty of fuse, and when the powder blew up, he was crouched down safely in the bush with his companion. The roar of the explosion beat against the muddy hills as the wagon disintegrated and pieces of lumber and steel were thrown high, wide and handsome. The noise must have carried some distance.

When Jim pulled his finger out of his ears he commented, "That's a load of wire the Talbot crew will never be able to stretch."

Bronc smiled and said the wire looked just like a big ball of string. "I got the itch creepin' over my ol' carcass to become a real powder monkey. Blow up somethin' else—like a drift fence, maybe."

"You got somethin' there, Bronc."

"I got brains, young 'un!"

They went for their horses and Jim told Bronc that the next step was to move into the Jones' spread for keeps. Bronc nodded and said the sooner they did that the better.

When they reached a rimrock ledge on the way, they saw the wagon team heading for the Heart Nine. The horses knew their way home, which was just as well for them, because they were without a rider. Shortly afterwards the men caught sight of the teamster making his way towards Branding Iron on foot and across the muddy hills.

Jim said, "He's leavin' without his rifle or pistol, must be in a hurry somewhat."

Bronc shrugged his shoulders and laughed.

They continued to ride across the hills, two men subject to the same pressure. Jim's Bucking Horse cattle, were across the basin along the northern foothills, grazing on thin brown grass. He was thinking of the problem they presented as he looked at the blue skies that held not a single cloud. Indian summer had come to this high northern range. According to his uncle, there might be a month of warm weather before winter really settled in.

Jim remarked, "Stay nice weather, Bronc, and we can head for Canada."

Bronc turned on his stirrups, sharp blue eyes glistening. "Them cows ain't fit to move, Jim. They gotta have rest to give them a chance. Nothing under a week at least."

"We can wait."

"The weather might pen us in."

Jim did not reply, being busy with his thoughts. Whether he wintered in Milk River, or drove north into Canada he would still have plenty of worry.

He had sent one of Len's riders to talk to the Mounties on the line about moving his trail herd into Canadian territory.

They drew rein, for the Jones' farm lay below them. Jim looked at the henhouse and barn and blacksmith shed.

"Smoke comin' out of thet shed," he told Bronc.

Bronc said, "Let's light." They got down and Bronc untied his field-glasses which he focussed on the outfit. When he put them down he said, "Two broncs tied by that straw stack back of the barn, Jim."

"The Talbots anticipated us," Jim said.

Bronc leaned back and fumbled in his vest pocket for a plug of chewing tobacco. When he got his cud adjusted he asked, "Got one stick of powder left, haven't we?"

"We've got a couple, Bronc."

"One to scare 'em," Bronc said, "an' one to blow them up if they don't scare. . . ."

Jim looked at the muddy earth. "Right you are. I'll slip around the rocks and come in against the shed."

Bronc said, "I'll cover you."

While Bronc squatted and watched the shed, Jim untied the dynamite sack. He adjusted two fuses and stuck the dynamite in his belt.

"Be tough on you if somebody shot you in the brisket, Jim. Watch yourself."

"You'll inherit my belt buckle," replied Jim with a smile. "Catch it on the way down."

But Bronc was deadly serious. "Go

careful, son. That girl has worried eyes and she doesn't deserve more trouble."

Jim cracked back, "She'd find another stiff within a week."

Soon Jim was moving downwards, darting from boulder to boulder, in his advance to the spread before him. The wind was warm against the sandstone and he began to sweat. Carefully he plotted each successive move, for he had to keep himself hidden. Bronc wasn't kidding about what would happen to him if a bullet found the dynamite.

For a moment he crouched behind a boulder, and glanced upward. He couldn't see Bronc, so he swung his attention back to the Jones' farm and made his way to the safety of yet another boulder, directly behind the site where the house had once stood. He was just in time, for a bullet passed just above him and then ricochetted off a rock.

Jim instinctively ducked.

From up the slope, Bronc Thomas' rifle roared. Jim heard the glass break in a window and hollered, "Good shootin', Bronc."

"Me an' the boys'll get them" Bronc shouted back, voice weak against the distance.

Jim smiled. Bronc was a smart one. Pretending he had help up there on the ridge, to give the Talbot men inside the blacksmith shop the idea they were outnumbered. Jim wondered how many men were in the building as he called, "Come on out, with your hands high."

"Come an' get us, Buckin' Hoss man."

Jim hollered back, "I'll dynamite you out."

"You ain't got no powder!"

Jim replied, "We got you surrounded. My men are on the ridges with orders to kill. Mary Jones has authorised us to take over her homestead."

"We got orders to hold it and kill if necessary, Texan."

Jim cocked his head, trying to identify the voice, but it hardly sounded like one of the brothers. He was about fifteen yards from the shed when he lit a fuse and waited before tossing the dynamite. The move cost him a bullet in the leg and he staggered as it hit him. For a moment it felt as if it had cracked the bone, and then he realised he had been wounded in the calf. He saw the dynamite drop to within ten feet of the shed, and then a startled yelp came from within the structure.

Those inside had realised their danger, and almost at once, a couple of panic-stricken Heart Nine riders, discarding their rifles as they ran, came into sight. The powder ignited, and as it blew up, the shed went over on its side and the gunmen dived for the ground. The air was thick with dust and fumes as Jim hobbled over to them.

Bronc appeared leading Jim's horse and he looked highly satisfied. "So you flushed the two skunks from their hole, eh?" It was then that he noticed Jim's condition and said, "So they winged you."

"They legged me," Jim corrected.

"But it ain't busted, otherwise you

wouldn't be able to walk on it." Turning to the captives he ordered them to put their hands behind their heads if they wanted to live a little longer. "One move outa either of you, and I'll pump plenty of lead into you," he warned.

The men sat down as ordered.

Jim rolled up his trouser leg. He had a blue hole in his calf. Bronc looked at it and said, "We'll get you to the doc in town."

The wound did not hurt very much. But it made his leg sort of numb. Bronc went into the barn where he found turpentine and clean bandages, the latter evidently an old sheet torn to strips.

"Must've kept them in there to treat sick work hosses," he said.

When the old trail driver poured turpentine into the wound it really hurt. Jim leaned back, leg extended, lips tight, while sweat popped out on him. Finally the bite left. Bronc bound the wound tightly.

Jim stood up, even walking a few steps.

"Thet turpentine will kill infection," Bronc said.

"Almost killed me."

One Talbot man said, "For Gawd's sake, let me git my arms down. My arms are dog tired."

"What'll we do with them?" Bronc looked at Jim.

Jim spoke slowly. "Sheriff Harden claims he wants a hand in this Milk River range war. He can have these two gents with my compliments."

"Mine too," Bronc added.

Within a few minutes, they were heading toward Branding Iron, with the two gunmen riding ahead of them. Jim did not put his weight on his wounded leg. Because of the tight bandage the wound had stopped bleeding. He only hoped it would not keep him out of the saddle.

Jim didn't like the idea of having to leave Mary's place unguarded, and wondered if he and Bronc had not moved a little too soon when they had found it occupied. Perhaps they should have waited and got some help before trying to take it.

He asked Bronc if Broken Nose had not said that he aimed to ride over to the place with Mary.

"That was what I figure they had in mind, when we left the ranch."

"Let's hope they do that," Jim said. Shortly afterwards however he suggested to Bronc that the oldster ought to head back. "We got to hold that spread if we want to get Len's cattle back across the drift fence."

Bronc however, could not be persuaded. He was determinted to stick to Jim. He took off his hat during the course of the argument and ran his gnarled hand across his bald head.

"No Buckin' Hoss man rides alone on this range," he asserted.

"I can take these two into town easily enough," Jim answered.

"No man rides alone," persisted Bronc.

In the end Jim gave up. He knew that once Bronc had made up his mind that there was nothing to be done. Jim realised, too, that there was some point about what Bronc had said.

"Let's push on into town and get back to Mary's place as quickly as possible, before the Talbots get wise to the situation," Jim suggested.

"Can you ride at a lope."

"Sure, let's go."

It was tough and painful sledding for Jim, who was in some pain, but he stuck it out and kept his place with Bronc just behind the horses of their captives.

18

Wild Guns

HORSE braced, Bowie Talbot rode down the hill, heading toward his new drift fence. He was more than satisfied, for he felt he had the Rathburns where he wanted them. Within a few days the drift fence would be completed, one wire stretched across what had been, until a short time before, open cattle range.

With this up, his crew would then string the other two wires, putting a barrier of shining barbwire across Milk River valley. With Chick and Mike squatting on the Jones' property, he had again out-manoeuvred and outguessed the Bucking Horse men.

Suddenly he thought of Lester Jones. Jones had run out of the burning house, and his bullet had killed him. The thought was not pleasant. It sent a shiver along his back, making his flesh crawl. Harden was a bulldog, despite his illness and now, more than ever, he would want to discover the truth of how Jones met his end.

He came to where his crew was stringing wire and putting down diamond-willow fence posts. Ole looked at him, a streak of mud across his wide and bland face.

"We get the fence in, Bowie."

Bowie ran his eyes along the posts and wire and then asked, "Where's Knife?"

"He rode toward town. That wagon load of wire should have got here by now."

Bowie Talbot nodded, "Driver prob'ly stuck around town a while to chin with thet girl in the store. He's sweet on her."

"We need the wire, Bowie."

"I'll check on it." Bowie Talbot said, and turned his bronc. He was thinking of Knife. His brother had been on the bad end of a couple of deals lately.

Ole said, "Did you hear two explosions?"

Bowie Talbot drew rein. "I heard somethin' roar when I rode out of the hills." He fed his bronc spurs, setting him to a hard gait toward the Jones' farm.

As he rode into the yard at a fast clip he saw the ruined blacksmith shop and hollered, "Mike! Chick!", but got no reply. He ran into the barn, was greeted by silence, and then returned to the wreckage, looking for tracks. He saw blood on the ground, he knelt and a crafty look came over him, lighting his harsh face.

When the two riders came into the yard, Bowie was on his feet, hat off as he spoke to Mary Jones. "Howdy, Miss Mary."

She said, brusquely, "Good morning."

Bowie Talbot looked at Broken Nose. The wide face of the dour Sioux resembled a sphinx.

Mary said, "I'll trouble you to stay off my property, Talbot. From here on, I don't want a Heart Nine man to ride onto my land, or set a boot on it. Is that clear?"

Bowie smiled. "Very clear, Miss." He kept watching Broken Nose, for the Sioux's eyes were as wary as a hawk. "Did you sell out to the Buckin' Hoss outfit?"

"I have sold to nobody."

Bowie said, slowly, "If ever you want to sell—"

"I do not want to sell."

Bowie nodded, eyes idle. Where in the hell were Chick and Mike? He noticed that Mary was looking at the blasted-down blacksmith shop.

"What happened to it?"

Bowie Talbot shrugged, said, "Wind must've blowed it down." He turned his bronc, a wryness in him. Ole had heard two explosions back in the hills. One had knocked down this blacksmith shop. What had the other accomplished, and where had it taken place?

He headed for Branding Iron and on the way found the spot where the dynamite had knocked the wagon to kindling.

He gave the place a hard and quick glance, then the thought hit him that again Jim Rathburn had come out on top. As he rode along Bowie had a feeling that his influence and power in the valley was on the wane. He had played his cards craftily, but perhaps the time had come for the heat to be really turned on—for nothing less than open warfare.

As he made his way towards Branding Iron, Bowie tried to piece together what had happened at the Jones' place. It was evident that somebody had got the drop on Chick and Mike, the two riders he had sent in to take possession of the place, and it was more than likely that Jim Rathburn had been active again.

If he had collared the Heart Nine men he would no doubt run them in to Branding Iron, but if they had managed to escape, Bowie reckoned that they might already have taken a run-out powder rather than face him or Knife. As Bowie rode on with his brow furrowed plenty was happening and had happened in Branding Iron that he was soon to hear about.

Events were moving fast.

Linklatter had spent the previous night in his office thinking and drinking. Hitting the bottle assuaged his nagging anxiety and, occasionally, he had slept a little, head on one side. When dawn broke he reached for the bottle again, but this time the whisky couldn't dull his fears. He was in danger and knew it only too well.

Time slipped by, but at last a man entered by the back door. "They blew up my rig," he said. "I'm not goin' back to the Heart Nine. In fact, I'm gettin' a hoss and lightin' out. I've had enough of Milk River."

Linklatter nodded. "Maybe you're doin' the right thing for your skin," he said with a sneer.

"That suppose to mean I'm scairt of the Talbots?"

"They'll kill you."

"I'm not afeared of those jokers."

Linklatter's thick lips showed a cynical

smile. "Now who the hell you think you're lyin' to, fellow?"

"Talbots owe me wages—"

"I'll not pay them. Go out to the Heart Nine and collect!"

The driver started forward. The .45 lifted from the open drawer in the land locator's desk and steaded on the driver, who suddenly stopped.

"Collect your own wages!"

The man looked at the gun, lifted his eyes, said, "So long, you skunk. You're as dirty as the Talbots."

He went outside, boots grinding on wet gravel. Slowly Linklatter lowered the gun. The feel of the bone handle, the heaviness of the .45 gave him confidence. The man who made the first gun made all men the same size. That was an old saying. He decided not to run. He had made the Talbots what they were and if he used his head he could make their outfit his own.

He got to his feet and took another drink. Perhaps, after all, Jim Rathburn was his chief danger and not the Talbots, and he was the one to be removed, if it could be done. Linklatter guessed the brothers would be along shortly to check on the driver who had failed to turn up, and he was willing to pit his brains against them if not his gun.

He grabbed the bottle for another swig, put it down unsteadily and then stepped out of his place into the street. He was just in time to see Chick and Mike ride in followed by Bronc and Jim Rathburn.

When Jim espied Linklatter he recollected the land locator's threat to kill him.

During the ride in Jim had done some hard thinking. The struggle against the Talbots were no longer a matter of desultory if violent encounters—it was all or nothing and he who hit first hit twice. Looking at Linklatter, Jim realised that here was a man who was not only his enemy and dangerous, but practically a partner of the Talbots. He had got the deeds for the brothers and had helped to settle their nominees on land over which the drift fence was now going up.

As Linklatter stood there expectant,

Jim decided that the time for a showdown with him had arrived. He said to Bronc, "Watch my back for me, amigo."

Bronc looked quizzical and said, "I don't get you, Jim."

"That gent over there is Linklatter."

Thomas had heard the name and understood. He told the Heart Nine men to dismount, and as they did so Chick asked, "What's goin' on?"

"Lead," said Bronc tersely and both men legged it for a wall where they could stand and watch the drama that was about to unfold. Someone suggested sending for Harden—"that is if he's around. He never seems to be there when you need him."

"He'll come late," Bronc said.

Bronc Thomas watched, gun in hand. Jim Rathburn did not leave his saddle; he moved his bronc parallel with the sidewalk. He was about twenty feet away from Martin Linklatter.

"You claimed you'd kill me," Jim said.

Linklatter wet his thick lips. He was cold and completely sober now.

"I said that and I meant it," he answered.

Jim shifted slightly, favouring his good leg. Saddle leather made its mystic creaking sound. "Come at it, then," he said.

Linklatter turned, as though to walk away, and Jim relaxed, but suddenly and treacherously Linklatter was turning, a cat on boots, and his gun roaring. He shot with too great haste however and missed, and Jim's answering bullet hit him below the heart. Linklatter grunted like a wounded bear. It was as though an invisible fist had smashed into his ribs. He looked at Jim and his great eyes rolled. His mouth opened and he roared in pain and fear as again he pulled the trigger of his .45. The bullet hammered down into the muddy street, and lifted a futile shower of small pebbles and mud. Then Martin Linklatter heeled over in the street, over the spot where his bullet had struck Montana earth.

Jim Rathburn holstered his gun, a cold fear inside of him. He had shot down a man whom he hardly knew. Jim turned his bronc then, for a horse had been ridden into the street, and its rider was Knife Talbot.

When Bronc asked Jim if Linklatter was dead he did not reply, but kept a close watch on Knife. The latter had drawn rein a short distance away and, after a glance at Linklatter stretched out in the mud, he asked, "What happened?"

Jim replied, "He pulled a gun on me just as he was pretending to walk away but, unluckily for him, I didn't fall for the trick and he came out the loser."

Bronc chipped in, "I've seen that move tried a few times. Move away and then whip round with a gun in your hand."

Talbot didn't answer for a few seconds. When he did he seemed almost to be talking to himself. "His job was through and it was time for him to move on." His eyes suddenly hardened and he added "Still, he worked for the Heart Nine."

Jim's reply came swiftly. "Takin' it up, Knife?"

For the second occasion Harden intervened between Jim and Knife, this time with a shotgun. The sheriff had barged out of a building, lifted his gun and shot fast and hard. Both men thought he was firing at them and ducked, but Harden actually was ploughing the bullets into the ground. It achieved its purpose though.

"No fight," he rasped.

Jim turned to him, grinning. "You handled that pretty good, sheriff. You had me scared."

Knife simply said, "Hell."

The sheriff's gun moved in a wicked gesture. "Talbot, into the saloon with you, and Rathburn, get off that bronc."

Jim explained, "I got a bullet hole in my leg. I have to get off slow."

Sheriff Harden replied crisply, "Stay in the saddle, then." He looked at the doctor who was beside Linklatter. "Dead?"

"He's still alive."

Harden spoke to a couple of onlookers and they helped carry Linklatter into the doctor's office. The big man sagged in the belly, like a broken mattress. Knife Talbot stood in the doorway of the saloon, watching. Harden looked at the two Heart Nine men.

"What about these two fellows?"

Jim said, "They squatted illegally on the Jones' farm. We came in and they opened fire on us and we drove them out. One of them shot me through the leg."

Harden said, "The girl will have to prefer charges."

"She will. Take them to jail."

Harden turned to Chick and Mike and said, "Down to the jail with you, and no monkeyshines." He looked up at Bronc Thomas. "Ther'll be a coroner's hearing over this shooting."

Bronc said, "Linklatter opened up the gunplay."

Sheriff Harden turned his attention to Jim once more. "I'll see you later. Better get Mary into town to file charges against these two. I can't hold them long on your say-so, Rathburn."

"You're wasting your time."

Harden's eyes glowed, dark and feverish. "What do you mean?"

"Twice you've walked in between me

an' Knife Talbot. The third time you won't be able to hold us back."

Harden's eyes were brittle. "War, eh!" he said.

19

Barbed Wire

BOWIE TALBOT looked at Sheriff Harden. "What if Linklatter dies?" he asked coarsely. "Does that mean you'll file a murder charge against Jim Rathburn?"

Harden played with a pencil. "Not necessarily, Bowie. If the coroner's hearin' says it was self defense, then Rathburn goes free."

Bowie looked at Knife. His lips showed a cyncial lift. "Rathburn man, all the way," he told Knife. "We might jus' as well holler down a well. Let's move, cowboy."

"Bought and paid for," Knife said.

Harden said nothing. His eyes had narrowed, and his lips trembled a little. He watched them walk out of the door. Big men, men of purpose, men of the saddle, men of guns. This was the way he catalogued them. Because he tried to be just and impartial they accused him of being corrupt. But he had long ago schooled himself to that kind of insult.

The Talbots walked past the window, boots making sounds on planks. They met the doctor in front of his office. He was going out to eat, and was gruff.

Bowie Talbot asked, "Linklatter?"

"Not too good."

"He'll die."

The doctor put his key in his vest pocket. "We're all going to die, Talbot," he said. "Some of us will just die ahead of the others. Flip four bits, and read the sign either way."

He went down the street without another word.

The brothers entered Linklatter's office and Knife settled himself in the agent's chair saying, "He won't sit here again, although he ain't dead yet."

"We can do without him now," answered his brother. "He's best out of the way, and if he takes too long in dyin', we might be able to push him on a little."

"Help him through the Pearly Gates, eh?"

"Boot him through," replied Bowie with a brutal laugh.

Knife looked at the safe. "Well, that dinero in there now belongs to us. We'd better raid the safe before the sheriff does legally, which he will do as soon as Linklatter shoves off."

Bowie went over to the safe and Knife from the swivel chair watched him turn the dial. Except for the sound of the tumblers the office was silent. After a while he shook his head and said he had fumbled the job.

"Have another go," urged Knife.

Again, Bowie Talbot worked the dial. This time, after much manoeuvring, the door opened. Knife glanced at the contents and said nothing. Bowie gave the interior a long and speculative glance.

"Everything packed nice and handy," he said as he slammed the door and looked at his brother. "Maybe he wasn't as Simon Pure at that."

"He had his ideas," Knife said. "And now, by Gawd, we'd better get some ideas, or we'll be out of Milk River valley pronto—on the outside lookin' in!"

"Don't talk like a chump, we own the drift fence. We have about two thousand head of ol' Len's Buckin' Hoss cattle behind that fence—on land we claim."

"They'll come after them, Bowie!"

Bowie Talbot turned, almost snarling. "Dammit, that's what we want, Knife! Make them come to us! We've gone to them too often. That drift fence will suck them in, and then it will be all over."

"Thet fence will never git built if they blow up our wagons like they did thet one today."

Bowie stopped pacing and stood silent. "If thet teamster hadn't hit it out of the country we could have got him to testify against the Rathburns and then Harden would have to act against them."

Bowie said, "Now the girl an' Broken Nose hold down the Jones' farm. We could run them out come dark but the whole country would know we did it, and if the girl stopped lead—well, it would be curtains for us."

"Hemp," Knife said, "hemp."

The conversation between the brothers was interrupted by a Heart Nine man who put his head in the back door. "Linklatter is just the same," he said.

Bowie said, with a grin, "Keep bringin' us the good news."

The rider looked from one brother to th other. "One of the boys found the team wanderin' homewards. No sign of the driver, though."

Bowie answered, "Looks as if he took it on the run. I'd like to get my hands on him for a few moments."

When the brothers were alone once more Knife picked up a gunny sack, looked it over and then said, "Get the safe open again."

Bowie did so without any difficulty, and they took everything out of it and filled the sack, the neck of which Knife secured with a piece of string. "It'll be good if he comes back and finds his safe looted," he mused.

"I'll get him with these," Bowie said and held up his big, calloused hands. "These will squeeze the life out of him and nobody will be the wiser that he didn't die from Rathburn's bullets."

Knife said, "My job—"

Bowie said angrily, "You've bungled everything so far! You'd bungle this job, too."

Again, the hired hand looked in. Bowie asked, "Where is Linklatter?"

"At the hotel."

"Which room?"

"I don't know. They took him to the hotel, though."

Bowie answered, "Drift around, keep your ears and eyes open, and your mouth closed."

"All right, boss."

The man left, and the brothers looked at each other. Finally Bowie said, "Now is the time to make a move."

"I'll check ahead of you."

Knife went outside, crossing the street

toward the two-storey frame hotel. He went into the lobby, and as nobody was behind the desk, he turned the thick register on its swivel and read the last notation: Linklatter, Room 202.

Knife Talbot climbed the stairs, a weight on him. He went down the corrider and found 202 and knocked. A woman's voice answered and he went in, stepping around her as she tried to block his way in.

"The doctor says nobody can see him."

"He's my friend."

She stood aside. Knife moved over and looked down at Linklatter, who lay with his eyes closed, lips opened slightly. Pain and loss of blood had done their work, putting across the wide face a look of stupidity. Linklatter had changed a lot in the last hour or two, so much so that the transformation startled Knife. Linklatter was a ghastly colour, and his eyes remained closed. He was not even aware of the presence of the visitor. Knife caught a sudden odour, and knew it was the smell of death. He stepped back into the hall and the nurse followed him.

"He's close to death, eh?" he asked.

"You never can tell. We have to have faith."

On the way back to the land locator's office Knife pondered on the possibility of getting rid of the nurse for a few moments. Linklatter would take very little to finish him off, but the presence of a watcher was a stumbling block.

Bowie Talbot looked at him as he came in, eyes probing his brother's swollen face.

"Room 202," Knife said. "Upstairs."

"I know the hotel. He got the nurse with him?"

"Yes."

"We gotta git shut of her."

"I know that," Knife said. "But how?"

Bowie said, suddenly, "Come with me," and his face showed a sudden lift. He and Knife went down the street with Knife wondering what lay on his brother's mind. They circled and came to the alley behind the hotel. Tin cans and garbage pails, and a cur digging in an upended barrel. The dog did not hear them for he had only his end sticking out of the barrel. Bowie kicked him and knocked him against the inside. The dog came out with a yelp and ran down the alley.

"You had no call to do that," Knife said sourly.

"Wish it had been Jim Rathburn's rump stickin' out, an' I'd've booted him even harder."

They went up the stairs that led to the second storey of the hotel and reached the wall where Bowie opened the door of an empty room. "I want you to stay in here," he said to his brother.

Bowie could see that Knife had not yet understood his plan and he took him over to the window. Below, an easy drop, was the roof of the adjoining building. It was flat and tapered off at the end, and from there it would be an easy job to jump into the alley.

Knife looked at him questioningly and Bowie said, "This is what I want you to do. Give me a chance to find a hiding place near Linklatter's room, then step out into the hall fire your gun at the ceiling and then dodge back into this room and get away through the window. It will be easy."

Knife nodded, "That should bring the nurse here right enough. It's a smart plan."

"Give me three minutes to get set, and, as soon as we draw the nurse away, I'll go into Linklatter's room and look after him."

Knife pulled out his watch and at the same time asked, "How are you going to get away?"

"Same as you, out on the roof."

Bowie went down the hall, opened the door of a room opposite, and, finding it empty, slipped in and closed the door after him. Nobody was around and he crouched down and looked through the keyhole. Then, suddenly, came the roar of a gun. There was a sound of running feet and Bowie saw the nurse dash out of the room, down the hall, and out of sight.

At once Bowie opened the door and in

a few strides was in the room where Linklatter lay. The injured man didn't move until Bowie grasped him by the throat. He was incapable of struggling, but before he died he opened his eyes and looked at the face of his murderer. Satisfied with his grim task Bowie rubbed his hands across the dead man's neck, as though to erase the red marks left by his fingers and then ran across the hall. It was empty. He went through the window, on to the roof and dropped into the alley.

Knife came out of a shed, his grin twisted and sardonic.

"Died easy," said Bowie.

Knife said huskily, "Let's get out of this alley sharp."

"Why the hurry?" Bowie demanded. "Every man has a right to walk down here."

"Guess that's right. No need to show our hand."

A few minutes later they were back in Linklatter's office and they had not long been there when one of their men came running to tell them that the land locator had just kicked off. His heart had given out, according to the doctor.

Bowie said, "Well, I'll be damned! His heart just gave out, eh?"

The man nodded. "Nobody was with him. Dangest oddest thing, too, somebody shot holes in the roof of one of the rooms, and the nurse ran down there to investigate. When she came back Linklatter had turned in his chips."

Knife Talbot cut in with. "What the hell do you mean by sayin' somebody shot up a hotel room?"

The man explained. "Sheriff thinks some kids snuck in there to raise hell. Dunno who did it, 'cept it was young-uns raisin' hell."

Bowie Talbot nodded slowly. His smile was only for Knife Talbot. "Now Sheriff Harden will have to file a murder charge against Jim Rathburn," he said.

Knife Talbot nodded.

FTN17

20

Hangman Range

MARY was at the Bucking Horse home-ranch, hanging up some washing, when Sheriff Harden rode into the yard. Mary spoke to Squaw. "That's the Sheriff, isn't it?"

Squaw nodded.

Mary's knuckles were cold from hanging up the washing. She found her hands trembling. "Linklatter must be dead," she said quietly. "That's why he rode out here."

Squaw's face, wide and impassive, showed nothing. She picked up the empty washtub and started toward the house, hips waddling as she moved.

Harden drew rein, and said, "Where is Jim Rathburn, Miss Mary?"

"Out on the range, I think."

Harden leaned back, reaching in his

vest pocket for his cigar. He bit off the end, leaned forward, match cupped. "And where's Len?"

"In the house."

Harden dismounted, and then he coughed, his body bent at the waist. Mary waited and Harden looked up with, "Sorry. Lately that cough has hit me unexpectedly." He started toward the house, bowlegged but slender. Mary ran and caught him and asked, "What is wrong, Sheriff?"

He kept on walking, but said, "Linklatter. Dead."

"Oh, Lord, what next?"

Harden stopped, then. "Range war," he said. "They'll slit that drift fence."

"When did Mr. Linklatter die?"

"About an hour ago."

Mary said, "And you have a murder charge against Jim?"

Sheriff Harden spread his long fingers. "I wanted to let it ride. Act when a coroner's inquest had investigated the killing. But the county attorney says I have to jail Jim until the jury has been convened."

"He won't go to jail."

"He will, if I get hold of him."

Mary said, "You'll have to kill him first, Harden."

Harden looked sharply at her. "You seem to know a lot about him, Mary. And he hasn't been on this range long."

She said, simply, "I love him."

Harden looked at her, marked the flush on her face, and had his own memories. This job was a thankless job—you walked the street no man's friend, and every one's potential enemy.

"You will be happy with him, Mary," he said, and went into the house.

Squaw came out of the kitchen, wiping her hands on a towel. "I hear," she said. "Now he argue with Len. You ride with news to Jim."

"I'll warn him," Mary said.

"Sheriff smart man. He follow you, girl."

"Not me," said Mary with rare determination.

Mary wasted no time. Within a few minutes she had her horse, Sonny, under saddle and led him out the back door of the barn so that she could not be seen from the house. Broken Nose was down at her farm, and Bronc had ridden out of town after Jim had shot Linklatter. The old trail boss had told her and Len about the fight. Jim had left for the hills because, Bronc explained, he did not want to be involved in a dispute with Harden.

As she rode along Mary hoped that old Len would in some way hold the sheriff on the home ranch until she had got to Jim. It was essential that he should know what the situation was and she urged her mount along, riding into the cold wind; somewhere she had heard that, in order to shake off pursuers, a rider should ride in water; therefore she rode along the bed of Beaver Creek for almost a mile. She came to the edge of the hills and rode into them, following Tank Coulee. Gradually the terrain lifted, moving upward from the level of Milk River valley, to become a rough country of boulders and brush.

She expected her herd to be in the vicinity of Tank Coulee, but it had moved north across the basin, and it was two hours later when she rode into the make-shift camp on Frenchman Creek. By now Sonny, despite the chilliness, was sweating, and lather hung from his bit. Jim saw her and spurred out to meet her, leaving the herd.

"Mary, what's the matter?"

"Linklatter died. Sheriff Harden came into the ranch, looking for you. I rode out to warn you."

She watched his face. She saw the boyishness leave it, and a hard maturity take its place. She did not know he could be so tough.

"I did right when I jumped outa town." He talked slowly and quietly. "But Harden said I'd be free until the coroner's inquest was held."

"He had to change his mind. The county attorney issued a warrant for your arrest. He has to serve it."

"He has to find me to serve it," Jim said.

Bronc Thomas loped up, face pinched with cold. They told him what had happened. For a moment silence held the group.

"You gotta lay low for a while, Jim," Bronc said, "we need you here, not in jail."

Jim nodded. Mary looked at the Texas cattle. They were grazing along the rim of the hills, trying to find feed. But the grass, such as it was, was sparse and stringy, and there was little nourishment in it. The thought came to her that maybe Jim would push north despite the nearness of winter and the danger of the northbound cattle-trek.

"Where you goin'," Bronc Thomas asked.

Jim said, "I got to be where you can reach me easy. I don't want to hang to the foothills, for he'll look there. I don't want to kill Harden. I want my trail clear. After we rip out that drift fence, I'll go to Harden and give myself up, but we have to hit that drift fence first."

Mary thought, Oh, Lord, protect them. . . .

Bronc said, "Them two skunks—them Talbots—they'll hunt you, too. There'll be open season on a guy named Jim Rathburn."

"You cheer me immensely," Jim said, grinning.

A cow bawled. Mary decided to change the subject, for this talk was making her nervy. "You're not—driving north, this fall, Jim?"

Jim shook his head. "We couldn't make it. I got a report back from the Canucks. We have to establish ourselves somewhat before moving in cattle, the Mounties say. But come spring we'll head north."

"If we have any cattle left," Bronc Thomas said sourly.

Jim said, "Again, you cheer me up." He looked at his foreman. "I know where I'll go."

"Where?" Bronc asked, watching him.

"To Mary's farm."

Mary said, "It's a good place to hide." Bronc leaned back, hands wrapped around the fork of his saddle. Then he smiled and said, "Always hide out in a place where they figger you wouldn't go. Harden will never look for you there. He'll ride the high ridges."

Mary said, "We'd better go."

Jim looked back at his herd. "Take the riders into the home ranch. Let the Texas cattle stray. Len's cows have the Buckin' Horse iron on their right ribs; our trail brand is on the left side. Come spring round-up we can cut out our stock easily enough. Move the men into camp and arm them and get ready."

Bronc nodded and said, "Take it easy and ride a light saddle."

Bronc rode back to the herd and Mary and Jim turned their horses towards the Jones farm. They moved into the lowland, broncs matching strides, the Montana earth building its sounds under the hoofs of their mounts. Although the cotton trees had lost their foliage their branches, barren yet strong, lifted into the cold wind.

Jim got the impression that snow could not be far away, and that this time they would be facing a real winter, not a preview of a season that could be terribly hard on man and beast alike. He had plenty to worry about, apart from this fresh development. The range was overstocked, hay continued scarce, and he had very little money. But the cattle would have to get along as best they could. When he thought about Linklatter he was certain that no jury would put him on the spot. The land locator had threatened him to others and had then lost a gun duel he had provoked. All the same Jim had no intention of being locked up while an official investigation was made. That would suit the Talbots too well. With him in jail, the Bucking Horse crew would be without a leader, and that was something that had to be avoided.

As they rode into the high brush along Milk River they could hear the sound of the water. It seemed to say *Man stays here a while but the river stays forever.*

Mary said, "This is where I leave you, Jim."

"Don't worry, I'll be all right at your place."

"Be careful, honey."

"I will. When a girl like you, Mary, waits for a man, no bullet in the world can kill him."

At once he knew he had said the wrong thing. He saw Mary's face blanch with fear. He longed for her, and peace and quiet for ther love to blossom, as he realised that he had found the one girl in the world. In this mood of tenderness he moved his horse closer, put his arm round Mary and kissed her. They clung together, each aware of the danger that lay ahead.

After Mary had left Jim did not seek open range again, for he was too close to the Bucking Horse ranch and he guided his mount along a trail through the buck brush.

Mary met Sheriff Harden within three

miles of the ranch. He was moving across the plain, heading for the herd on Frenchman Creek. When he saw her, he pulled over and looked at her with eyes what told her that he knew where she had been and for what purpose. For all his quiet demeanour, Mary sensed that he was a man of courage and determination and not to be trifled with.

"Is there any use in riding to the Bucking Horse herd?" he asked at once. She shook her head and returned his cool stare.

"I'll ride that way anyway, and let's call it doing my duty. You could be arrested, you know, for helping my prisoner to escape."

Mary smiled slow and tantalisingly. "Could you prove that?" she asked.

The sheriff knew only too well what Mary had suffered by the death of her father and what she might still have to face. He admired her courage, and realised she deserved the happiness she hoped to find with Jim Rathburn.

Leaving the girl's question unanswered he nodded to her before riding away.

She watched him move towards the mouth of Frenchman Creek, across the basin. He moved into space and was soon lost to sight. She looked towards the west, and, from a butte about three miles away, she saw the thin ribbon of smoke. Jim was telling her he was there.

She rode towards the Bucking Horse ranch. Len, in his wheelchair, came towards the barn, face showing anxiety. She slipped her latigo loose and put her saddle on the rack and took the bit off Sonny.

"Jim?" he asked.

She said, "Harden won't get him." They walked toward the house, and she shoved the wheelchair, and she felt, suddenly, that she belonged here—she was Jim's, and therefore she belonged to Len, too. It was a good thought. Squaw waited in the doorway. She rolled Len inside. The fire blazed in the rock fireplace and she stopped the chair there, hands over the fire.

"Where did he hole up?" Len Rathburn asked.

"At my farm."

Squaw said, "Best place. I get whiskey." She came back with three glasses. "Drink, Mary."

The whiskey burned but it tasted good and Mary felt it move into her blood. Suddenly she kissed Len on the forehead. Then she turned and ran to her room down the hall.

Len said slowly, "Jim has found a good woman, Squaw."

"He has, Len."

21

Rifles

WHEN Jim Rathburn rode into the yard Broken Nose came out of the barn with a rifle under his arm. Jim said, "Linklatter died."

The Sioux's face gave nothing away. "How's the leg?" he asked.

"Gettin' along okay. I aim to hide out in this vicinity. Harden has a warrant for me, and the charge is murder. Mary tells me there's a Buckin' Horse rider here with you?"

"He in barn."

"I take his fresh bronc. He can take my hoss back to our spread. Then if Harden snoops he finds my horse there, not here."

The cowboy threw his saddle on Jim's horse and rode away. Jim hurriedly saddled the fresh cayuse. He checked his

Winchester. "I'm takin' to the hills, Broken Nose."

"Gotta keep movin', Jim."

"Harden is sick. He won't ride far. And he operates without a deputy or under-sheriff, they tell me."

"He have deputy until a few days back."

"What happened to him?"

"Too much troubles. He ride away, they say. Cold boots!"

Jim Rathburn checked his outfit. He had a blanket tied across his saddle-shirts, some jerky-beef in his saddlebags and three boxes of .30-30 cartridges and one of .45 shells, too.

"See you later," he said, and rode south towards the hills.

"Report back come night," Broken Nose said.

Jim rode on, reaching the foothills. Finally he was on the rimrock. Below him stretched the broad length and width of Milk River valley. A scene of desolation, now that fall had stripped the trees; the ground was barren except for the grey of sagebrush, the green of greasewood. The river was a line marked by dried cottonwoods and leafless box-elder trees. But he had no eye for this desolate beauty, he was on the alert for potential enemies.

He saw Sheriff Harden ride to the Jones farm. Through his field glasses he watched the lawman search the buildings. Harden even went into the root cellar, dug out against the hill. Jim smiled at this. This done, Harden headed for town, and on the way Jim watched his meeting with Bowie and Knife Talbot, coming out of Branding Iron. Behind the Talbots came a wagon loaded with wire and other equipment. The sheriff stopped and talked, and Jim wished he knew what was being said. He was sure they were talking about himself and in this surmise he was correct.

Bowie Talbot asked, "Any trace of your man, Harden?"

"He jumped the country."

Bowie looked at his brother, and his grin was cynical. Knife regarded the lawman coldly.

"That's too bad," he said sourly.

Harden shot him a quick and hard glance. "Still accusin' me of ridin' in the shadow of Len Rathburn, eh?"

Knife shrugged his shoulders and with calculated innocence remarked, "You don't have to jump on little Knife that quickly. I wasn't accusing you of anything, sheriff."

Harden knew that whatever he said would not convince the Talbots. They had long ago made up their minds about him and they couldn't be reasoned with. He was now sure that one, or both of them, was responsible for the tragedy of Lester Jones and that his death was not suicide. He looked at the stationary wagon and the driver high in the seat, with his rifle alongside him. It was loaded with barbed wire that was meant to change the character of the range, but men, he reflected, remained the same, greedy, fearful and dangerous.

"Drift fence wire?" he asked. Bowie Talbot nodded.

Harden lifted sunken eyes. "You got

some of Len Rathburn's cattle on your side of the drift fence, they tell me. About two thousand head."

Bowie said slowly, "They drifted on our side in the storm. Fence wasn't built then. Now they're behind the bob-wire."

"You got it all strung?"

Bowie said, "One wire, all the way."

"Not all the way," Harden said. "The Jones farm blocks you."

Bowie Talbot's face pulled down mean and savage. "Sheriff, I'll lay it on the line. No Buckin' Hoss round-up is to be staged on Heart Nine grass. Tell your pals that if they come after them two thousand odd head they'd best make it a Winchester round-up!"

"You can't steal their cattle."

"I haven't stolen 'em!" Bowie Talbot leaned forward very quiet and careful to pick the right words. "They drifted, remember? That ain't rustlin'—when you rustle a cow, you drive her off her range."

"I know that."

"Accordin' to law, they owe me a fee

for each cow behind my fence—a stray-fee. That's the law, and you know that."

Harden said, "Hell, I can imagine Len Rathburn payin' you stray-fees—or his nephew forkin' over, for that matter!"

"The fee," said Bowie, "will be cheap. Just three bucks a cow. . . ."

Harden said, "They'll cut them cows with Winchesters, Talbot."

Bowie's mouth showed a hard smile. Knife fingered the scar on his jowl. A horse stirred, mud moving under his hoofs; a work-bronc moved, a tug chain made its clanking sound. The driver listened, and across the hills a cow bawled, the sound moving along the edge of the rocks.

"Tell them to come on with their rifles," Bowie Talbot said. He had found out what he wanted to know, so he looked at his brother. "Ride along, Knife." To the teamster, "Follow us, fella."

Harden watched the Talbots move off and sat his horse awhile, thinking. He would liked to have known where Jim Rathburn could have been found, but it was a certainty he could not be far away with his herd in Milk valley and range war just round the corner.

At that very moment Jim was riding down a wide coulee, angling towards the road he knew the wagon would come along. He pushed to the north-west, coming in at a tangent to intercept the load of fencing supplies. He was going to give the Talbots something to keep them occupied for a little while.

He left the gully and rode up a slope, his mount slipping in the mud, but quickly regaining its balance. He reached the top, dismounted and reached for his Winchester. Then, he hid his bronc securely at a spot over the crown of the hill, before climbing onto a boulder, where he lay flat, legs spread and the gun at his shoulder and waited.

At last the wagon came round a bend in the road and he allowed it to travel a little way before he wished himself "good shooting" and let the hammer drop. His target was a spool of wire, directly behind the driver's seat, and as the bullet slapped home the driver hollered with surprise and fear, dived off his seat, and left the reins hanging on the brake.

Jim sent in another shot behind the team and this turned them into runaways, despite their heavy load. As the horses took fright the rifle fire galvanised the Talbots into action and, as their broncs wheeled round, Jim saw the flash of Bowie's pistol. The range was however, too great for such a weapon and when Jim sent a shot towards Bowie he grabbed his rifle and dived for the ground with his brother. Their broncs took it on the run.

Jim had an eye on them and the other on the wagon which quickly hit a pot-hole, lurched and went over sideways. The team broke the double-tree pin and loped wildly off, kicking at their traces.

The Talbots were in a dangerous predicament. They had lost their mounts in the surprise attack and they didn't know how soon they might become casualties. Eventually they got up and made a dash for safety and the last Jim saw of them was when they disappeared in a coulee, hotfoot in pursuit of their loose mounts. For good measure Jim sent a few shots after them and then slid to the ground and ran for his bronc.

He hit leather and loped up the coulee, heading back to the rimrock. Later, he reached the rimrock and saw far below him two specks which told him that the Talbots had at last caught up with their horses.

He circled to the west, dipped down again and came into the Milk River basin where he dismounted and waited, squatting close to a big rock.

The day was dying and the air was cold. Within an hour the Talbots rode by, heading for the Heart Nine. He grinned as he followed their movements, for they were less than a mile away.

Jim felt that he ought, somehow, to let the brothers know that he had been on to them and the opportunity came when he espied a Heart Nine rider coming down off the hills and heading for the home ranch.

Jim guided his horse behind some

bulberry bushes, and when the rider went by rode out behind him with his rifle across his saddle.

"Jes' a minute cowboy," he called.

The man turned his horse on hearing the summons, hand on his holstered gun. He looked at Jim from under craggy, iron-grey brows.

"What is it, Rathburn," he asked.

"I want no trouble with you," said Jim.

"Why then did you stop Pinky Jergens?"

"I want you to pass on a little information to the Talbots, your bosses. Tell them it was me who held them up a little while back."

Jergens nodded. "Okay, I'll do that," he said. "One of them will kill you," he added as an afterthought.

"I'm hard to kill," Jim assured him.

22

Lawless Range

BOWIE TALBOT looked at the cowboy. "So this Rathburn gent stopped you just to let us know he was the one who peppered us, eh? Now that you've told us this little bit of entertaining news, make tracks."

"I jus' thought—"

"Get out!"

The cowboy left, anger scrawled on his face. Bowie turned to his brother, seated in a chair in front of the fireplace.

"The last straw, Knife."

The scar showed on Knife Talbot's jowl. His black eye glistened. But he said nothing as he watched his brother.

Bowie said, "We'll get every hand out on the drift fence. Patrol it from here to hell an' back."

"It's asking a lot to cover all that ground."

"We'll patrol it."

Knife looked back at the fire's glowing embers. "How about Rathburn? We cain't hunt him down. Too many hills and he can change hosses."

"Forget him."

Knife smiled almost wistfully. "Wish I could," he said.

Bowie said, "You ride south and I'll head north. They'll hit at the Jones' farm, or else I'm off my bat by miles. We'll concentrate our strength at the centre of the fence, with guards out."

Knife nodded. "About Six-Mile line camp, then?"

"We meet there," Bowie said.

Knife said, "We need Chick and Mike."

"In jail," Bowie replied. He buckled on his spurs, fingers angry with the straps. This done to his fancy, he crossed the room and took two boxes of rifle cartridges from the mantelpiece. "The men are armed and have reserve cartridges. Still, there's a couple cartons of .45 and Winchester shells in the storeroom. I'll see Sig and he can take them to Six-Mile."

Knife said, "A cold wind out, Bowie."

Bowie Talbot whirled, glaring at his brother. "You might not feel it for long," he said cynically, lips curling. "They might have you under six feet of earth soon, and they'll get you there—unless you pull out something better against Jim Rathburn than you have so far!"

Knife was on his feet, moving towards his brother. "Harden stepped between us each time, you low-lived devil! Don't throw that in my face or I'll choke you with my bare hands."

Bowie Talbot allowed his smile to widen. Then he said, "Doggone it, Knife, you still have the old spirit left, eh? Thought mebbe you'd lost it . . . Show it when the Buckin' Hoss tangle horns with us!"

Knife Talbot stopped, hands knotted. His eyes moved over the face of Bowie

Talbot. Then he loosened, the tension breaking; his hands unclasped.

"Always baitin' me, Bowie. Someday I'll call you and kill you!"

"Save it for the Rathburns."

Bowie left, rifle in hand, saddlebags in the other. Knife watched him go to the corral and throw his loop. Bowie boasted he had never missed roping a horse in a *remuda*. The saddle-stock ran around him as he made his cast. Knife saw him drag in an empty loop and wondered if this was not a bad omen for his brother. Then Bowie threw again and caught a black around the head; he led him in, saddle him, and headed out into the wind.

Bowie rode away from the ranch house set there in the gaunt cotton woods. He had the feeling that events were coming to a head, that the coil was running out and soon everything would be decided in the struggle for power. He and Knife had both made their play for Mary Jones. Now she was Jim Rathburn's woman. Down in Branding Iron people were gossiping. A Texan had cut out two other

Texans in Mary's favour. Bowie did not want the girl as bad as he disliked being beaten. Beaten, and talked about. . . .

He gave his mind to more urgent matters. How and where would the Rathburns hit? He knew the Bucking Horse crew would strike at the fence. Back of it were about two thousand head of Len Rathburn's cattle. Rathburn would not pay impound fees except in lead and gunpowder. Bowie looked towards the south. A rider had left the Heart Nine and was riding towards the southern foothills. He knew it was Knife.

Knife Talbot rode with the wind. He had his gunbelt strapped outside of his mackinaw and a Winchester rode in the saddleboot, stock up and handy for a man's grip.

Knife, too, was thinking of Mary Jones.

All the range knew about Jim Rathburn whipping him, there at the Jones' farm. And it happened because of Mary. . . . Knife wanted her, and his mind played with the image of her, and he tasted her promise. But by the same token, deep inside was a voice, and this said she would never be his. This logic prevailed, and greed and revenge came in, filling the void. Greed for this Milk River range; revenge against Jim Rathburn. With these emotions came another fear. But most of it pointed towards his brother. Bowie it had been who had done Lester Jones to death, and Bowie it had been who had choked the life out of Martin Linklatter. There was consolation in these thoughts. A man never knew at what time the pendulum would change and swing against him.

The fence-crew was quitting work and was loading the wagon with augers and wire. Knife Talbot said, "Make your camp at Six-Mile tonight."

"What's the idea?"

"You heard me. Swing around and camp at Six-Mile."

"Trouble, Knife?"

"Trouble. Where's the other crew?"

"Over the hill, I guess."

Knife Talbot rode over the sun-tanned hill with its dead grass. Always a cowman, he glanced at the grass: short and grazed-down. Tough winter if snow got too deep and it hung around zero too long. Still, they had some feed in the stacks—they had cut hay along Milk River. Bluejoint hay, good hay. Not much, though, for the crop had been short.

Ahead of him was a wagon, inching over the hills. He caught it and said, "Turn around, men. The camp is Six-Mile, not Wagon Bend."

"Why Six-Mile, Knife?"

"Trouble ahead."

The driver turned the wagon, moving against the wind. Knife Talbot sat on a butte, his horse quiet under him; he looked at the fence. All the posts were in. One wire was already in place and two more were going onto them. The crew had worked hard and had done a lot of work.

Now let them do work as good with Winchesters and pistols, he thought. What the hell was Harden doing down in town? He would have liked to have known.

Harden, as a matter of fact, was in his office looking at a list of names he had compiled. His handwriting was hard to read, even to himself. The list complete, he went to the first man whose name appeared at the head of it, Clem Abbott.

"You're my deputy," he said.

Abbott was wrapping a package in his grocery store. His wife, who was waiting on a customer, stopped and watched. Abbott did not look up.

"Len Rathburn is my friend, sheriff, but the Talbots use my store, too, and I don't want your deputy badge."

"Afraid of losing trade, eh?"

Abbott snapped the string he was tying. "Afraid of losing my life, you mean. Maybe you can conscript me sheriff. I don't know, but there's an old saying that you can lead a horse to water but that you can't make him drink."

Harden replied, "I need help."

Abbott looked at him for the first time. "I'd like to help you. But there'll be guns out there and, frankly, I don't want to get killed. This business concerns the Bucking Horse and the Heart Nine outfits and they must settle it between themselves."

"I have a sworn duty."

"I know. But you'll have to get along without me."

Harden hesitated and then turned and left the store without another word. He got to work on the names he had listed, but got the brush-off from four of his fellow townsmen. Soon, he discovered that everybody knew what he was after, and he found that at house after house, at which he called, everybody was conveniently engaged elsewhere, at least that was what the wives of the men he wanted to speak to told him.

Never before had so many people in Branding Iron been so busy on projects which called them out of town.

When he reached the last name on the list he had still not found a deputy and he knew he had wasted his time. He returned to his office and was not too surprised or too disappointed. Nevertheless, he had hardly expected rebuffs from everyone without exception.

He sat in his office, the fire warm in the stove, and watched the day die. This was the hour he liked best. Shadows moved in from the higher hills.

At last Harden got to his feet and reached for his rifle. He stood and looked at the dull blue of the barrel. He had owned the weapon for many years. Each time he moved out of town, each time he had a job to do, the rifle went with him. It was his third hand, his most deadly hand.

His dead wife had called it that, and she had hated it as women hate violence and blood-shed and the sorrow that followed. He thought of her for a moment, and realised that her memory was always with him. Why had she to die and still always be with him? Really he was a man with two faces, one he turned towards the world, the other to his soul!

Suddenly, he, too, hated the rifle.

Nevertheless, when he went down the street, the rifle was under his arm, barrel pointing to the ground. He met several whose aid he had vainly sought, but he looked at them without anger. The fact that they placed a bigger value on their own lives than he did on his own did not lessen them in his eyes.

He could understand their aversion to gunplay and their desire to live in peace and without violence.

Harden saddled a black gelding—a tough-barrelled, short-legged mount, good for the hills and rough slants. He put the rifle into the saddle-holster, with the stock protruding and then packed some cartridge boxes into a sack which he tied across the saddle.

The hostler, an old bent man, studied him. "Ridin' alone Harden?"

The sheriff nodded and hoisted himself up. "That's right," he said.

"Everybody's a'scared?"

Harden answered, "Maybe not afraid, Joe. Maybe just sensible." He touched the horse and it walked jauntily through the town, out towards the hills. Night was approaching and with work to do Harden quickly urged his mount into a fast gallop. He knew what he had to do, even if all the details were not yet quite clear.

From a hill, he saw the Heart Nine men gathering at Six-Mile and realised the plan he had was more than feasible—Six-Mile was in the centre of the drift fence area, and each end was equidistant from the log linecamp. Harden looked towards the Jones' farm. With a wry smile he remembered that he was supposed to be hunting for Jim Rathburn, but there was a bigger job ahead.

He circled and came into the yard of the Bucking Horse ranch. It was dark when he dismounted and stalked towards the house. He pounded on the door and heard someone say, "Come in."

Len Rathburn greeted him. He looked pale and weak and Harden saw that time, and his wound, had hit him hard. The gruffness had left the lawman as he asked, "Night ride ahead of you, Len?"

Rathburn looked at him with fathomless, ageing eyes. "I don't follow you, sheriff," he answered.

"I think you do, Len."

Rathburn replied. "No, that's not so. Jes' tryin' out my pins to see if they have any strength left."

"Rifles stacked in the corner, Len."

"Always there."

"Horses saddled along the corral fence, Len."

Len Rathburn looked at him. Lamplight made his eyes mere shadows. They were old friends, and knew each other well. Len Rathburn understood he was not fooling the lawman, and Sheriff Harden knew that he, in turn, was not fooling Len.

"Always have night horses, Harden."

Their eyes met and held. Harden lifted his thin shoulder. He felt he could have done with some warmth and some hot grub although he realised that such comforts were not for him until the job was done.

"Got a bottle, Len?"

"In the dresser drawer. Second one."

Harden moved across the room, spurs making tiny sounds; the drawer slid open with a squeak. He fingered through some towels, found the bottle. It had companions, arranged in a row.

"Hidin' it from Squaw, eh?"

Len said, "A woman always hounds a man, be she red, white, yellow or black."

"You've had experience enough," Sheriff Harden said. He did not open the bottle, put it in his coat pocket. "Good night, Len."

"You runnin' off with the whole bottle?"

"I am." He stopped at the door, eyes serious. "Hope you're alive come dawn."

"The same to you, Harden."

Harden found his stirrup and got up. He turned the horse and sent another glance around the Bucking Horse grounds. Men moved, there was the rattle of gear. Maybe somewhere in those shadows was young Jim Rathburn?

Harden thought of Mary Jones.

He looked at one of the windows of the ranch-house and saw the image of a woman against the blind. She was sitting in front of a dresser combing her hair.

Even as he glanced, she got to her feet, and moved beyond the reach of his eyes.

He rode on, thinking of a drift fence.

23

Dark Night

JIM RATHBURN rode into the barn, got out of the saddle, and said, "Throw my kak on a fresh bronc, Joe." He halted in the doorway. "Be sure the sack is there on the fresh hoss. And the rifle, too."

"They'll be on your saddle, Jim."

Jim went towards the house, boots grinding on the gravel walk. He walked past Bucking Horse men into the house and said, "They're leavin' Six-Mile, Len."

Len Rathburn stared with narrowed eyes. "They aim to rush us, eh?"

"Harden did it," Jim said. "He snooped around and they knew he would report to us, so they pulled their men out."

Mary and Squaw stood in the doorway

leading to the kitchen. Jim looked at Mary and saw her concern. Squaw was solid and wide and dependable. "We can't let them lay siege to these buildings," Len said. "They'd burn 'em down."

"I figured that. We'll ride out."

Len pulled on his sheepskin overcoat with the aid of Squaw. Mary still stood in the doorway looking at Jim.

"We'll meet them about Black Butte, eh, Jim?"

"That's more than likely," Jim said. "Harden went toward the Six-Mile camp. He passed me in the hills."

"The boys?"

"Waitin', outside."

Len had his rifle. He looked around the room and then glanced at Squaw. "Be good," he said.

"I be that."

Jim spoke to Mary. "I'll see you later."

"Later, Jim."

Len hobbled out, carrying his rifle, and Jim with another look at Mary, followed his uncle outside. He could still see her standing there in the yellow lamplight, girlish and pretty. They went out into the raw cold moonlight. Buildings were dark shadows grouped across the cold and sullen earth. Snow was falling, pushing towards the earth. The thermometer was dropping. Fingers would be cold on rifles, on short-guns

Len said, "To your hosses, men. We ride to Six-Mile."

Boots found stirrups, and bodies lifted to settle between forks and cantles. Jim thought he might have to help his uncle mount, but somehow Len Rathburn got into the saddle alone, his pride lifting him. Jim mounted his fresh horse and pulled the Winchester out.

"What's the plan?" somebody asked.

Len Rathburn grunted, "Shoot to kill. Jim is the boss."

Jim said, with a crooked smile. "Thanks for the honour. When we see them, we stretch out and give them some lead."

Len growled, "And a hundred dollar bonus to any man who kills a Talbot."

"I need some new boots," a rider quipped.

Somebody laughed, not too spontaneously. Jim looked back at the ranch house. The lamp had gone out. He thought of the two women there: one red, one white. Sisters, though, in trouble.

They strung out, riding fast and came to the hills, and the house below them was quickly lost. Jim took the lead with Len riding beside him. He glanced at his uncle and saw that even under the thin moonlight his face was pale. Snow fell harder and thicker, and the thought came to Jim that maybe a blizzard would stop them. but it would only be a postponement. Jim found himself liking this high northern range, and he hoped his cattle would pull through. A Texan, always thinking of his cattle, he thought, smiling to himself. After a few minutes, the wind began to lessen.

They rode through the hills, and Jim knew the country by this time. He kept thinking of Mary Jones, and her softness and her strength. She helped him now, as every woman helps her man, in times of duress and danger.

A rider angled in from the south-east and rifles went onto him. It was Broken Nose who said, "They drift this way, Jim. Still comin'."

"Where do we meet?"

The Sioux gave the matter some thought. Men watched him and waited to hear his opinion and finally he said, "By Black Butte, maybe."

"Where we figured," Len said.

"They more of them than us," answered the Indian.

They rode on, slowly this time, and then the high ridge known as Black Butte lay ahead, crowned by snow. The riders came to it and Jim said, "This is it," and his men halted, staring at the horsemen ahead who had seen them and had drawn rein about three-hundred yards away.

Jim said loudly, "Buckin' Hoss riders, Talbots."

Bowie Talbot hollered back, "We ride for your spread, and we're Heart Nine men, Rathburn."

Jim replied, "This place is as good as any."

A rifle bullet screamed overhead, and men went out of saddles, rifles in their hands. Jim went down, shouting, "Get to the rocks on the butte," and he saw Len dismount. They left their horses, running bent over, firing as they ran, heading for the boulders that stuck black snouts out of the snow along the wide base of Black Butte.

Jim saw that the Heart Nine men were also now on foot. There was a mix-up of running horses, most of them with bridle-reins down, and snow was being churned beneath hoofs. Jim saw a Bucking Horse man fall and it looked by the way he hit the ground as if he was dead. Then, they were behind rocks, firing over boulders.

Suddenly Len bawled, "For God's sake look!"

A rider had come out of the snow-filled night and pulled up between the opposing sides. He raised his hand and shouted "This is Sheriff Harden and you men have got to stop this fight. Get back to your ranches at once."

No one replied, but there came the ping of a bullet over on the Heart Nine side and Harden doubled up in the saddle and then lurched over and fell to the ground. His horse moved away, but Harden lay prone.

Jim murmured, "If that wasn't suicide I don't know what is."

Harden's death seemed to galvanise everyone into a frenzy. The scream of bullets and the smell of cordite filled the air as each faction threw everything they knew into the fight. The Heart Nine men lay on the ground and made poor targets. As Jim pumped lead at them he thought about Harden, trying to do his duty and knowing that he would be killed. After another hot exchange of fire Jim decided that fresh tactics were called for. He moved around to each man and told him to wait for a signal to get to grips across the snow with the Talbot gang.

A brief lull came, as Jim expected it would, and suddenly he jumped to his feet and yelled, "Come on boys, let 'em have it!" They raced out from behind the shelter of the rocks and their rifles began to talk at close range. As guns roared in the dwindling space Jim heard Bowie shout, "Get at 'em, you so-called tough gunmen."

Heart Nine fighters obeyed and in a flash two waves began to converge. As Jim crouched over, running, he saw that his uncle was down, sitting in the snow. He still had his rifle and said, "I stopped one." At that moment Jim saw Bowie coming towards him, but before he had time to fire at the Heart Nine leader, a shot came from Len's rifle.

Bowie stumbled in his tracks, dropped his gun and then spun over. He lay silent and still, dark against the snow.

Jim heard Broken Nose exclaim, "Len, he get him. He wait for that." The Indian was like a coiled spring, and he fought as a Sioux fights, crouched and deadly.

By one of those ironic twists of Providence Jim escaped death just afterwards because of the wound he was carrying in his calf. In the thick of the fight his leg suddenly gave way and he sprawled over at the very moment that Knife Talbot got a bead on him and fired. The bullet whizzed harmlessly over and Jim grabbed his Winchester and sent one into Knife. He went down holding his body in agony and his cry of despair was heard by other Heart Nine men.

One of them shouted, "They got Knife too. Let's get out of it." With the fall of the second of the Talbots the fight was virtually over and after a few desultory shots the Heart Nine men began to run, they wanted no more of it. Broken Nose, with a wicked gleam in his eye, asked Jim if their fighters should go after them but Jim said it wasn't necessary and that there would be no more trouble.

They went over with Bronc to where Len lay. He had a cigarette between his lips and said, "It's a long way from Texas to Montana. A man never knows really where he'll be buried. I'll tell that sheriff what a bum lawman he was when I meet him."

"It'll be a few years before you talk to him," Jim vowed.

"No," answered Len, "You're wrong Jim. I'm on my way out and know it. Squaw will miss me. I should've married her, I guess."

"You will, Len."

"Hell, she'd be a strange lookin' bride decked out in lace!" Gnarled fingers dug into loose snow. "Snow's different here than in Texas. Kinda rougher."

The fingers became still.

Jim got to his feet. It was hard to realise a man could die so easily.

Winter came like a ferocious enemy and hung on with tenacious grip. When the Bucking Horse outfit ran out its spring round-up wagon many head of cattle had perished and wolves and coyotes had waxed fat on their carcasses. After the fight at Black Butte, the Bucking Horse men had ripped out the drift fence, and following the death of Knife Talbot, Jim bought the Heart Nine outfit from the county with money Len had left him. The Talbots had left no heirs.

Knife had survived for almost a month, and, before he died, he cleared Jim of the murder charge and talked about other things as well.

One spring day Broken Nose was branding a calf, the smell of burning hair wafting strongly. He looked at his new boss, Jim Rathburn, and said, "Buckboard comin', Jim."

Jim coiled the rope he was using and waited in the saddle, looking across as the buckboard approached. Mary pulled the team up in front of him.

"How's the round-up coming, Jim?"

"Not too bad considering. We'll have a fine outfit here in a few years, but it'll mean plenty of hard work."

"Well, it's something to look forward to."

Jim spoke quietly and seriously. "Len wanted me—his next of kin—to have his cattle. He worked hard for the day when he could turn the outfit over to me. Now we'll work for the children we're goin' to have someday."

Mary nodded, her eyes on her husband.

"You sure look swell, sweetheart," Jim said.

THE END

Other titles in the Linford Western Library:

TOP HAND
by Wade Everett

The Broken T was big enough for a man on the run to hire out as a cowhand and be safe. But no ranch is big enough to let a man hide from himself.

GUN WOLVES OF LOBO BASIN
by Lee Floren

The Feud was a blood debt. When Smoke Talbot found the outlaws who gunned down his folks he aimed to nail their hide to the barn door.

SHOTGUN SHARKEY
by Marshall Grover

The westbound coach carrying the indomitable Larry and Stretch and their mixed bag of allies headed for a shooting showdown.

FARGO: MASSACRE RIVER
by John Benteen

Fargo spurred his horse to the edge of the road. The ambushers up ahead had now blocked the road. Fargo's convoy was a jumble, a perfect target for the insurgents' weapons!

SUNDANCE: DEATH IN THE LAVA
by John Benteen

The land echoed with the thundering hoofs of Modoc ponies. In minutes they swooped down and captured the wagon train and its cargo of gold. But now the halfbreed they called Sundance was going after it, and he swore nothing would stand in his way.

GUNS OF FURY
by Ernest Haycox

Dane Starr, alias Dan Smith, wanted to close the door on his past and hang up his guns, but people wouldn't let him. Good men wanted him to settle their scores for them. Bad men thought they were faster and itched to prove it. Starr had to keep killing just to stay alive.

FARGO: PANAMA GOLD

by John Benteen

Cleve Buckner was recruiting an army of killers, gunmen and deserters from all over Central America. With foreign money behind him, Buckner was going to destroy the Panama Canal before it could be completed. Fargo's job was to stop Buckner—and to eliminate him once and for all!

FARGO: THE SHARPSHOOTERS

by John Benteen

The Canfield clan, thirty strong, were raising hell in Texas. One of them had shot a Texas Ranger, and the Rangers had to bring in the killer. Fargo was tough enough to hold his own against the whole clan.

SUNDANCE: OVERKILL

by John Benteen

Sundance's reputation as a fighting man had spread. There was no job too tough for the halfbreed to handle. So when a wealthy banker's daughter was kidnapped by the Cheyenne, he offered Sundance $10,000 to rescue the girl.

HELL RIDERS
by Steve Mensing

Wade Walker's kid brother, Duane, was locked up in the Silver City jail facing a rope at dawn. Wade was a ruthless outlaw, but he was smart, and he had vowed to have his brother out of jail before morning!

DESERT OF THE DAMNED
by Nelson Nye

The law was after him for the murder of a marshal—a murder he didn't commit. Breen was after him for revenge—and Breen wouldn't stop at anything . . . blackmail, a frameup . . . or murder.

DAY OF THE COMANCHEROS
by Steven C. Lawrence

Their very name struck terror into men's hearts—the Comancheros, a savage army of cutthroats who swept across Texas, leaving behind a bloodstained trail of robbery and murder.

SUNDANCE: SILENT ENEMY
by John Benteen

Both the Indians and the U.S. Cavalry were being victimized. A lone crazed Cheyenne was on a personal war path against both sides. They needed to pit one man against one crazed Indian. That man was Sundance.

LASSITER
by Jack Slade

Lassiter wasn't the kind of man to listen to reason. Cross him once and he'd hold a grudge for years to come—if he let you live that long. But he was no crueler than the men he had killed, and he had never killed a man who didn't need killing.

LAST STAGE TO GOMORRAH
by Barry Cord

Jeff Carter, tough ex-riverboat gambler, now had himself a horse ranch that kept him free from gunfights and card games. Until Sturvesant of Wells Fargo showed up. Jeff owed him a favour and Sturvesant wanted it paid up. All he had to do was to go to Gomorrah and recover a quarter of a million dollars stolen from a stagecoach!

McALLISTER ON THE COMANCHE CROSSING
by Matt Chisholm

The Comanche, deadly warriors and the finest horsemen in the world, reckon McAllister owes them a life—and the trail is soaked with the blood of the men who had tried to outrun them before.

QUICK-TRIGGER COUNTRY
by Clem Colt

Turkey Red hooked up with Curly Bill Graham's outlaw crew and soon made a name for himself. But wholesale murder was out of Turk's line, so when range war flared he bucked the whole border gang alone . . .

PISTOL LAW
by Paul Evan Lehman

Lance Jones came back to Mustang for just one thing—Revenge! Revenge on the people who had him thrown in jail; on the crooked marshal; on the human vulture who had already taken over the town. Now it was Lance's turn . . .

GUNSLINGER'S RANGE
by Jackson Cole

Three escaped convicts are out for revenge. They won't rest until they put a bullet through the head of the dirty snake who locked them behind bars.

RUSTLER'S TRAIL
by Lee Floren

Jim Carlin knew he would have to stand up and fight because he had staked his claim right in the middle of Big Ike Outland's best grass. Jim also had a score to settle with his renegade brother.

Larry and Stretch: THE TRUTH ABOUT SNAKE RIDGE
by Marshall Grover

The troubleshooters came to San Cristobal to help the needy. For Larry and Stretch the turmoil began with a brawl, then an ambush, and then another attempt on their lives—all in one day.

WOLF DOG RANGE

by Lee Floren

Montana was big country, but not big enough for a ruthless land-grabber like Will Ardery. He would stop at nothing, unless something stopped him first—like a bullet from Pete Manly's gun.

Larry and Stretch: DEVIL'S DINERO

by Marshall Grover

Plagued by remorse, a rich old reprobate hired the Texas Troubleshooters to deliver a fortune in greenbacks to each of his victims. Even before Larry and Stretch rode out of Cheyenne, a traitor was selling the secret and the hunt was on.

CAMPAIGNING

by Jim Miller

Ambushed on the Santa Fe trail, Sean Callahan is saved from dying by two Indian strangers. Then the trio is joined by a former slave called Hannibal. But there'll be more lead and arrows flying before the band join the legendary Kit Carson in his campaign against the Comanches.

DONOVAN
by Elmer Kelton

Donovan was supposed to be dead. The town had buried him years before when Uncle Joe Vickers had fired off both barrels of a shotgun into the vicious outlaw's face as he was escaping from jail. Now Uncle Joe had been shot—in just the same way.

CODE OF THE GUN
by Gordon D. Shirreffs

MacLean came riding home with saddle-tramp written all over him, but sewn in his shirt-lining was an Arizona Ranger's star. MacLean had his own personal score to settle—in blood and violence!

GAMBLER'S GUN LUCK
by Brett Austen

Gamblers hands are clean and quick with cards, guns and women. But their names are black, and they seldom live long. Parker was a hell of a gambler. It was his life—or his death . . .

ORPHAN'S PREFERRED
by Jim Miller

A boy in a hurry to be a man, Sean Callahan answers the call of the Pony Express. With a little help from his Uncle Jim and the Navy Colt .36, Sean fights Indians and outlaws to get the mail through.

DAY OF THE BUZZARD
by T. V. Olsen

All Val Penmark cared about was getting the men who killed his wife. All young Jason Drum cared about was getting back his family's life savings. He could not understand the ruthless kind of hate Penmark nursed in his guts.

THE MANHUNTER
by Gordon D. Shirreffs

Lee Kershaw knew that every Rurale in the territory was on the lookout for him. But the offer of $5,000 in gold to find five small pieces of leather was too good to turn down.

RIFLES ON THE RANGE

by Lee Floren

Doc Mike and the farmer stood there alone between Smith and Watson. Doc Mike knew what was coming. There was this moment of stillness, a clock-tick of eternity, and then the roar would start. And somebody would die . . .

HARTIGAN

by Marshall Grover

Hartigan had come to Cornerstone to die. He chose the time and the place, but he did not fight alone. Side by side with Nevada Jim, the territory's unofficial protector, they challenged the killers—and Main Street became a battlefield.

HARSH RECKONING

by Phil Ketchum

The minute Brand showed up at his ranch after being illegally jailed, people started shooting at him. But five years of keeping himself alive in a brutal prison had made him tough and careless about who he gunned down . . .

FIGHTING RAMROD
by Charles N. Heckelmann

Most men would have cut their losses, but Frazer counted the bullets in his guns and said he'd soak the range in blood before he'd give up another inch of what was his.

LONE GUN
by Eric Allen

Smoke Blackbird had been away too long. The Lequires had seized the Blackbird farm, forcing the Indians and settlers off, and no one seemed willing to fight! He had to fight alone.

THE THIRD RIDER
by Barry Cord

Mel Rawlins wasn't going to let anything stand in his way. His father was murdered, his two brothers gone. Now Mel rode for vengeance.

RIDE A LONE TRAIL
by Gordon D. Shirreffs

The valley was about to explode into open range war. All it needed was the fuse and Ken Macklin was it.

A-1

ARIZONA DRIFTERS
by W. C. Tuttle

When drifting Dutton and Lonnie Steelman decide to become partners they find that they have a common enemy in the formidable Thurston brothers.

TOMBSTONE
by Matt Braun

Wells Fargo paid Luke Starbuck to outgun the silver-thieving stagecoach gang at Tombstone. Before long Luke can see the only thing bearing fruit in this eldorado will be the gallows tree.

HIGH BORDER RIDERS
by Lee Floren

Buckshot McKee and Tortilla Joe cut the trail of a border tough who was running Mexican beef into Texas. They stopped the smuggler in his tracks.

HARD MAN WITH A GUN
by Charles N. Heckelmann

After Bob Keegan lost the girl he loved and the ranch he had sweated blood to build, he had nothing left but his guts and his guns but he figured that was enough.